TORTURED

"You ever wonder, Luthor, what happens to everything you've learned when you die?"

The man shoved the chair away again, and this time it fell on its side. Luthor landed on his arm, and the pain was so intense that his entire world turned white for a brief moment. The kidnapper kicked him as hard as he could in the kidneys.

Luthor's breath left his body.

The man grinned. "If I decide to kill you here and now, there's no one to stop me, Luthor. I can take my time. Rather like you do when you decide to destroy someone. I can do it in one punch—"

And he brought his fist down on Luth[illegible] Luthor choke.

"—and one kick at a time."

The boot found Luthor's ribs again...

OTHER BOOKS IN THE SERIES

SMALLVILLE: STRANGE VISITORS

SMALLVILLE: DRAGON

SMALLVILE: HAUNTINGS

SMALLVILLE

WHODUNNIT

DEAN WESLEY
SMITH

Superman created by
Jerry Siegel and Joe Shuster

ASPECT®

WARNER BOOKS

An AOL Time Warner Company

WARNER BOOKS EDITION

Cover design by Don Puckey
Book design by L&G McRee

Warner Books, Inc.
1271 Avenue of the Americas
New York, NY 10020

Visit our Web site at
www.twbookmark.com.

Visit DC Comics on-line at keyword DCComics on America Online or at http://www.dccomics.com.

 An AOL Time Warner Company

Printed in the United States of America

First Printing: March 2003

10 9 8 7 6 5 4 3 2 1

For Kris, always
the mystery of my life

SMALLVILLE
WHODUNNIT

CHAPTER 1

Clark Kent had to hide the strangest things. It was the hottest day of the spring, and he hadn't even broken into a sweat. Sweating wasn't something a guy could fake, no matter how many strange powers he found himself blessed with. So, instead, he kept a slight distance between himself, Lana Lang, and Chloe Sullivan, hoping that they wouldn't notice.

They hadn't walked far in the ninety-degree temperature, but Chloe and Lana looked like they had wilted. Initially, Clark had suggested that they wait until later to walk up to the Franklin farm, but Lana shook her head.

She'd already waited too long to find Danny Franklin. Lana had been assigned to work with Danny on a lab project, but Danny hadn't been in school for three days, and no one was answering the Franklin phone. So Lana had asked Clark to go along with her to the Franklin place.

"I'm relying on you, Clark," she had said. "I don't want to go to the farm alone."

Clark agreed, of course, and Chloe, who had been standing nearby, had offered to drive. Lana had smiled her gratitude to both of them.

She hadn't said why she was reluctant to visit the Franklin farm on her own; after all, she had been friends with Danny Franklin longer than anyone else had. But Clark hadn't asked. He didn't really want to know.

He would accompany her, no matter how silly it seemed to walk to a farm in the unusual April heat wave. He never could say no to Lana Lang.

The humidity made the air heavy and thick, dampening the sounds of their footsteps on the gravel driveway that led to the Franklin place. Trees shaded this part of the walk. Sunlight came through the leaves in beams, making the shadows dark and welcoming in their coolness. Ahead Clark could see where the gravel driveway crested over a slight hill. They only had another dozen steps in the shade, then the road would be out in the open sunlight again.

Clark had never been this deep inside the Franklins' property. He'd only been to the gate, which was about a hundred yards behind them.

Chloe's car was parked there, blocked from coming up the driveway by the metal gate and a padlock that looked rusted. Clark had no idea why someone would lock a gate across a driveway when there was no fence on either side of the gate. Just ditches and weeds marking the line between the road and the open fields. Any truck could easily bounce down through the ditch and go around the gate to get to the driveway.

Chloe had pointed at the indentation left in the weeds and noted that the gate looked like it had stood open for years and had only recently been closed. Clark did not like the sound of that.

"Maybe the Franklins had a family emergency in Metropolis," Lana said as she tucked a loose strand of hair behind her ear.

"That still doesn't explain why they would lock the gate," Chloe said. "No one in this area locks gates."

Clark nodded his agreement. There was a gate at the edge of the Kent farm that could swing across the driveway, but Clark couldn't remember a time it had ever been shut. He had cut the weeds around it more times than he wanted to count, but he had no idea why it had ever been built. And he had never asked. More than likely the driveway gates in this part of Kansas were more to show ownership of a road than anything else.

"Maybe the Franklins just shut the gate to let delivery people know they were gone," Clark said.

"Maybe," Chloe said. "But I still think it's weird."

"Everything in this town is weird to you," Clark said, smiling at his friend and bumping his hip against hers.

"True," Chloe said. "Weird keeps things interesting, that's for sure."

They came out of the shade and into the open sunlight. Clark could feel the heat instantly, but it didn't bother him, not like it bothered the girls. He didn't know why it worked that way, but on days like today, he was glad it did. He made sure his steps were slow enough to match Lana's and Chloe's, since both of them seemed to be fighting the unseasonably warm day, and he needed to at least seem like he was as well.

A slight breeze hit them from the south, but not enough to take away the thickness of the air and the strange feeling Clark was having that they were heading into trouble.

"I don't remember hearing we were going to have summerlike temperatures," Chloe said, wiping her hand across her forehead. "Hope they have the fans working at school tomorrow."

"We're just used to the cold," Lana said. "Makes it seem warmer."

Clark smiled. "Yeah, we're going to think this is cool in August."

"Not likely," Chloe said. "I'll sweat just as much then as now."

"I thought girls didn't sweat," Clark said.

"That's right," Lana said, laughing. "We glow."

"You can glow all you want," Chloe said. "I'm sweating, and I hate it. Someday I'm going to move to Alaska just to get out of this stupid humidity."

"And take pictures of bear and moose and piles of snow?"

Clark asked, grinning at his friend. "You'd miss all the fun of Smallville."

"I'd miss the weirdness," Chloe said. "I wouldn't miss this heat."

They crested the top of the hill and stopped.

Below them, the Franklin farm filled the shallow valley. A large pond filled the right side of the valley, and the driveway skirted the left edge of the water, leading up to a turnaround area in front of the white house. Two large barns dominated the hillside behind the house. To the right a large area had been dug and tilled for a garden. There weren't any stakes, string, or identifying markers at the end of the tilled rows, so Clark doubted it had been planted yet. Right now he knew his mom was starting to plant their garden, and when he got home he was going to have to help.

No car sat in the Franklin driveway, and the barn doors were closed up tight. Nothing was moving.

"Looks empty," Lana said. She sounded surprised.

Clark wasn't—and he finally figured out why. The silence. Working farms were never silent in the spring. He should have heard an engine roar from a tractor or voices as people worked the fields.

And the smells were wrong, too. Right now, the Kent farm was filled with the pungent odor of fertilizer. Clark's dad used manure—saying it was old-fashioned, but the best. Other farmers used chemical brands, but even those smelled as awful as the cow dung did.

Silence and no stench. Closed barn doors, and no cars. Something had gone wrong here. He could sense it. And now that he was thinking like the farmer's son he was, he realized that no farm family left home in the spring, unless there was an emergency.

"Did Danny seem distracted to you?" Clark asked Lana.

"Lately?" she said. "Sure. First he was worried about

doing all his chores. Then his dad got laid off from LuthorCorp, so the family had financial worries."

"The Franklins always have financial worries," Chloe said.

"Yeah," Clark said. "Farm families generally do."

Lana gave him a sympathetic look, but he ignored it. He hadn't said that so Lana would feel sorry for him.

The Kents handled the financial troubles as best they could. But Clark could remember his father's reaction when Jed Franklin, Danny's dad, finally gave up full-time farming and got a job at LuthorCorp.

Do that, Clark's dad had said, *and you guarantee your farm's failure.*

But what choice does he have if they don't have any money? Clark asked.

A farm can always feed the family, Clark, his dad said. *Remember that.*

"Anything you can tell Mr. Phillips about the lab project?" Clark asked Lana. "Maybe get another partner to finish it?"

"It looks like I'm going to have to," Lana said. "I just wonder what happened. Danny didn't say anything about leaving town."

"Some people don't report to school when they go out of town," Chloe said.

"Danny talks to me," Lana said. "He would have mentioned something."

Clark fought the jealousy that rose in him. Danny wasn't Lana's boyfriend either. Whitney was, and he was off in the Marines. If Lana had been having a conversation about Clark, she probably would have said "He talks to me," in just that same tone.

But Clark had seen how Danny looked at Lana, had recognized it as a wistful look that often crossed his own face.

Lana was a lot more popular than she ever thought she was, but part of her charm was that she didn't realize just how appealing she was.

Chloe glanced at Clark. He knew how attuned she was to his moods, and she could probably sense how deeply this worried him. She wiped the sweat off her forehead and frowned at the farm.

"Well," she said, "I'm about as pitted out as I can be. Another few yards won't make me any grosser. We might as well go knock to make sure no one's there."

Clark smiled at her choice of words. He nodded.

Lana shrugged. "Might as well."

They walked the rest of the way down the hill in silence. Chloe took her camera off her shoulder. She had that look that said she had gone into reporter mode.

Clark used the time to study the house and barns, looking for any danger inside them with his special vision. He couldn't see any problems, and he knew there was no one home. Everything seemed to be in its place. Yet still the sense of something wrong didn't leave him.

At the bottom of the hill, the road tucked in near the large pond before moving to the turnaround in front of the house. The hills, the nearby trees, and the fields behind the barns made this farm feel very isolated. Even the slight breeze they had felt on top of the hill didn't ruffle the smooth surface of the water.

The buildings were well kept and looked like they'd been painted last summer. There was no trash in the yard and no tools left to rust. Tulips were starting to poke out of the ground in the front flower beds, and the small lawn was trimmed. Clearly Danny's dad ran a controlled operation here.

But Clark knew that money was really tight for Danny's parents. Since Jed Franklin's layoff, Danny's older twin sisters had taken part-time jobs around town to help out. Money was still so tight for them that Lana had even had to spring for the lab supplies she and Danny needed.

Since being laid off, Jed had been seen a number of times drunk and shouting nasty things about LuthorCorp. Clark had heard his parents talking about it a few times. His dad figured that Jed's anger would ease when the weather got clear enough to let him get back to work in the fields.

And from what Clark could tell from the neatly tilled rows, Jed Franklin had been doing just that. Only the tilling marks looked old and tamped down. Clark and his dad had started work a month ago, picking rocks, then tilling, and finally, just last week, covering everything in fertilizer.

Someone had clearly picked rocks and tilled, but the work had stopped there. And it looked like the Franklins had been on the same schedule the Kents were.

What would pull a farmer away from his farm right when there was the most work to do? It made no sense.

"Clark!"

Chloe's voice had a sharp bite to it. Chloe had stopped without him noticing, so he had to spin around.

Chloe was pointing into the water.

"What?" Lana asked, staring at where Chloe was pointing.

Something floated just under the smooth surface of the pond. At first Clark thought he was looking at a birch tree branch, the white bark almost luminescent in the brown water.

Then he saw blue fabric and realized that what he had taken for a branch was actually a white hand. It was about ten feet from the weeds bordering the road.

Someone was under the water.

Clark ran to the edge of the water and waded in. The water was shockingly cold, still holding its winter chill. The cold didn't bother him, but Clark hoped whoever was in the water hadn't been there long. He wasn't sure how much time the average person could be in water this cold and still survive.

The waves he created made the arm bob up and down. The hand peeked through the water's surface, mud-covered, dirt beneath the fingernails.

The water was chest deep and the mud on the bottom pulled at Clark's sneakers.

He reached the hand and pulled it upward. He knew at once the hand, and the body it was attached to, wasn't alive. And it hadn't been for a long time. The cold, slimy feel of the skin made him remember the time he had picked up a dead fish, kept too long in a cooler.

His stomach twisted, and he took a deep breath and held it.

He eased his grip on the slick skin and gently pulled. The body came to the surface right in front of him, facedown, bloated against the clothes it was wearing. Danny Franklin's blond hair floated around the head, brushing against Clark's chest.

"Oh, no," Lana said, sounding as if her heart had been broken. "Oh, no."

CHAPTER TWO

Blasted heat wave in the middle of April. Not only did it make a man uncomfortable, it also screwed up business in a hundred little ways.

Lionel Luthor adjusted his silk suit coat over his shoulders. Silk was not appropriate for ninety-degree days. He had summer suits for that sort of weather.

Not to mention all of the problems in the various buildings he owned around Metropolis. He had arrived at work this morning to find the heat still on. His secretary had called building maintenance, only to be informed that the maintenance supervisor was the only person who knew how to change over the system from heat to air-conditioning, and the supervisor was on a planned vacation until the following week.

It took two hours to find a way around that problem. Two hours in which Luthor cursed the old-fashioned building he usually loved. Even the windows in his office had swollen shut.

It was enough to make the most reasonable man cranky. And Lionel Luthor was not often a reasonable man.

He had business at City Bank and had spent the last three hours in their air-conditioned conference room. The cool air had taken the edge off his anger, fortunately, since an angry man was not a good businessman.

The meeting with the bank president had worked exactly as he had needed it to work. Lionel was leveraging a small-capital company named Stanley Feed and Grain into much larger capital. It didn't matter to him that in less than a month Stanley Feed and Grain would be shut down, its assets sold off, its long-term employees out of a job. This was business. The owners of Stanley Feed and Grain had sold him the controlling share of the company, and now he was going to use it.

If they hadn't wanted him to run their company the way he saw fit, they never should have sold him the controlling shares. Of course, the idiots had had no idea why he had wanted those shares. They would soon understand.

Sometimes Lionel Luthor saw his job as simple education. He was teaching inept businessmen how successful people worked.

His sense of satisfaction left him, though, as he stepped through the revolving door in the lobby. The door opened into a small glass security enclosure between the bank and the street.

The enclosure was as hot as his office had been.

Beside him, Hank Bender, the current chief of security for LuthorCorp, sighed. Hank seemed even more uncomfortable than Luthor was, if that was possible. But Hank was a big man, strong and muscular. He often looked like he'd been squeezed into his suits.

Today he looked like he'd been squeezed into his clothes before they were dry.

"Fluky weather, boss," Bender said.

"Uncomfortable, yes, fluky, no," Luthor said. "According to this morning's paper, Kansas occasionally suffers high temperatures in April."

"Must be real occasional because I don't remember it."

Neither did Luthor. In fact, he always thought the best time of year in Kansas was the spring. Winters were too cold; summers were too hot. He did his best to be away from Metropolis when the worst of the heat hit.

The city's large population and all that went with it, the

cars, the subways, the sheer hot air from too many conversations, seemed to increase the heat exponentially.

Bender pushed the glass door open for Luthor, and he stepped through. It felt like he was entering a steam bath fully dressed. Everyone seemed to feel that way. The crowd passing along the sidewalk struggled to maintain business dress. Most of the men carried their suit coats over one arm and had their sleeves rolled up. None of the women appeared to be wearing nylons, their bare feet swelling in shoes made for cooler temperatures.

Luthor shook his head. Through the crowd, he could see the limo, parked in the loading zone. The engine was running to keep the interior cool. Luthor had instructed his driver, Jerome Jenkins, to do that every summer. Jenkins, good man that he was, remembered it in this heat wave.

Luthor's bodyguard, Tony Kodale, had already left the bank, checking out the area as he always did, before signaling that everything was all right. Sometimes Bender took that job, but Luthor preferred to have Kodale do it.

Kodale seemed to have eyes in the back of his head—almost literally. Once Luthor had actually looked. After all, he'd seen stranger things.

As Luthor started across the sidewalk, Kodale pulled the limousine's passenger door open. Standard procedure, although Kodale should have waited a few more seconds. He was letting precious chill air escape.

People streamed by, none of them in their usual hurry. The heat was so thick, it felt like water, slowing down everything in its path. Even Luthor was walking slower than usual.

Bender moved slightly ahead of Luthor, opening a hole in the crowd. A tall man in a heavy overcoat hung out on the edges, a winter cap pulled low over his eyes.

Now that was a determined person—one who wasn't

going to let the realities of the day interfere with the way he'd dressed when he got up that morning.

Luthor shook his head as he stepped off the curb. The man in the overcoat bumped past Kodale, not looking at anyone. Kodale glared at him in irritation and started to say something, but his words sounded garbled.

Then Kodale's eyes rolled up, his shoulders slumped, and he dropped to the sidewalk, landing with a resounding crack.

Bender hurried toward him, then stopped as if he'd hit a wall. Slowly Bender crumpled to the sidewalk. There had been no shots, no sign of attack, yet two of his guards were down and out.

At that moment, the guy in the overcoat moved to the front of the car. He yanked open the driver's door. Jenkins toppled sideways. Apparently, he'd been unconscious the entire time Luthor had been walking to the car.

Luthor, knowing he was in trouble, looked over his shoulder for a way out. But the crowd had him penned in.

A hand roughly pushed Luthor in the back, shoving him at the open limo door. "Inside, Mr. Luthor."

Luthor stepped sideways, just the way his security team had trained him to do. Most people went forward or back, never to the side. He pushed against the crowd, hearing a man grunt as Luthor hit him in the stomach.

The hand grabbed Luthor's shoulder, holding him back.

Luthor tried to step away again, turning as he did so. A fine mist of spray hit him squarely in the face, stinging his eyes. He choked on the stench of orange—not like the fruit, but like orange soda pop left too long in the sun.

The world spun, the light of day started to dim. He tried to fight back, but his hands wouldn't move. His knees were giving way. He was going to end up on the sidewalk beside Kodale.

How could his security have been breached so easily? He had precautions for this. Safety net after safety net.

How dare these people attack him?

He struggled to maintain his consciousness, but he felt it slipping away.

Rough hands shoved him forward. His feet hit Kodale's sprawled body, and Luthor tripped, falling face first into the open limo door.

His face bounced against the soft leather seat. He tried to sit up, to move away, but he couldn't. He couldn't do anything. The sickly sweet stench of the spray seemed stronger in here.

Too strong.

The smell was the last thing his brain registered before he passed out.

CHAPTER THREE

It took Chloe nearly a minute before she remembered that she held her camera in her hands.

Lana was standing at the edge of the pond, hands covering her mouth. She'd cried out when she first realized that the body floating in the water had been Danny Franklin, and since then she hadn't made a sound.

Chloe was wondering if Lana was even breathing.

Clark still had ahold of Danny Franklin's hand. He was dragging the body to the side of the pond, ripples forming around them like rings.

Clark looked so heroic and so sad all at the same time, his tall broad form bent over the body as if he could protect it. The sun was behind him, making him glow, and he looked more than human, as if the light around him gave him an extra dose of strength.

That was what Chloe always relied on Clark for. His calmness, his personal strength.

The stench of rotted flesh filled the air, followed by something even fouler, like a swamp gas. Bubbles rose around the body, and now it was Chloe's turn to cover her face.

The smell was coming from Danny's corpse.

She wanted to throw up, and instead swallowed hard. If she was going to be a real reporter some day, she would have to be able to handle dead bodies, and everything that went with them, including the smells. Still, her stomach turned, and that was when she picked up the camera.

It was either look through the lens or lose the bland cafeteria pizza she'd had for lunch.

She focused the camera on Clark and took shot after shot,

trying to get the effect of the light, thinking about Clark and not the boy he was pulling ashore, the boy she'd spoken to not a week ago—teasing him about his crush on Lana Lang.

How come everyone had a crush on Lana, anyway? All she was doing was standing there, her long hair trailing down her back, her body shivering as if she were suddenly cold. She wasn't *doing* anything. Clark and Chloe, they were doing something. But Lana was just standing there. And it was beginning to bug Chloe.

"Hey, Lana!" Chloe said, surprised her voice sounded as normal as it did. "You got your phone?"

Lana's hand went to her book bag, then she turned, and Chloe thought she saw gratitude in Lana's eyes.

"Yeah." Lana walked away from the edge of the pond, digging in her bag as she did. "I guess we should call someone, huh?"

"The police," Chloe said. "We sure don't need an ambulance."

Hiding behind her camera, her finger clicking the shutter open and closed, the lens focused on Clark as he eased Danny's body to shore. Chloe felt stronger than she actually was. But if she brought that camera down, she'd have to face what she was seeing.

She had lost a friend. Not as good a friend as he'd been to Lana, but a friend all the same.

Chloe swallowed, and took a few more shots, glad she had her digital and not the school's expensive thirty-five millimeter. The digital gave her two hundred pictures, and she was probably going to use them all.

Lana had moved behind her. "Yes, this is an emergency," she was saying.

Clark had reached the shore, and he tugged the body past the reeds growing at the water's edge. Chloe took two more shots.

"It's Danny Franklin," Lana said. "He's dead."

Chloe's hand shook. She brought the camera down. Danny was wearing jeans and a denim work shirt. Had he been wearing that the last time she saw him? He didn't have a lot of clothes—or at least a lot of variety in his clothes—but he didn't wear the same thing every day either.

"I'm pretty sure he drowned. We're on the farm and he was in the pond and Clark just pulled him out . . . Clark Kent . . . I'm Lana Lang. Look, this is serious . . ."

Chloe made herself take a deep breath and really look at the situation. The pond wasn't that deep. Chest high on Clark who, admittedly, was outrageously tall, but still. Guys like Danny Franklin didn't drown in their family's pond, not in the place they'd grown up and played in and skated on and swum in. Guys like Danny were competent and composed and—

"Clark!" Chloe yelled almost before she realized she was going to say anything. "Clark!"

Lana stopped talking. Clark looked up. His face was pale, and he looked ill. Chloe couldn't remember the last time she'd seen Clark look ill.

"Don't do anything else. Don't touch him anymore."

Clark let go as if he'd been waiting for someone to give him permission. He backed away from the body. His clothes clung to him, and bits of algae hung off his jeans.

"What's going on?" Clark's voice carried across the pond. He sounded as unsettled as Chloe felt.

Lana was still looking at her, hand over the cell phone. A voice, faint and indistinct, squawked from the receiver.

"It's okay," Chloe said to Lana. "Get them out here."

Lana nodded and went back to talking on the phone.

Chloe walked toward Clark, clutching her camera at her side. As she walked close to the pond, she caught a whiff of the scummy water, mixed with that gassy odor she had noticed before, all of it overlaying the smell of decaying flesh.

Her stomach turned again.

Clark watched her. He held his right hand away from his body, as if he didn't want to touch anything else with it. Danny lay at his feet, immobile, his flesh so pale that it looked like it was made of ice.

"This is a crime scene, Clark," she said when she reached his side.

"You don't know that," Clark said. "He probably hit his head and fell in the water. He—"

"It doesn't matter." She should have thought of this before. She wasn't yet a professional reporter, and she wouldn't be until she did everything right. "He's too young to have died of natural causes. The coroner and the police are the ones who determine if this was an accident or not. And we just messed with it."

Clark closed his eyes for a moment, then opened them, nodding. "I screwed up."

"No," Chloe said. "It's not your fault."

"I didn't realize he was dead until I touched him." Clark grimaced slightly as he said that last.

Chloe looked down at Danny's body. She had noticed how different it looked, but she hadn't thought about how it would feel. Slimy? Cold?

Dead. Definitely dead.

"And then all I could think was that I had to get him out of there." Clark was watching her, as if she was the one who was going to yell at him.

"That's just human, Clark. Anyone would do that. But we'd better not do anything else."

Clark nodded.

Then Lana folded her phone over and stuffed it in her

book bag. "They're coming," she said. "They want us to wait."

Of course they did. Lana, Clark, and Chloe were witnesses.

The smell was stronger here. Chloe wasn't sure how long she could hold out against it—how long she could continue to ignore the fact that she'd liked Danny, who was now lying dead at her feet.

Chloe looked toward the house. Silent. Empty. The barn doors closed. She hefted the camera in her hand.

"We've got a little time before the police arrive," she said. "Anyone want to come with me? I'm heading down to the house."

"Chloe," Clark said in that tone of his. It was not quite disapproving, and there was fondness in it, but he was trying to stop her.

"Clark, I am a reporter," she said. Or she would be when she had her reactions under control. "And no reporter would pass up the chance to investigate just a little bit more. Especially since I have my camera."

"What do you expect to find?" Lana asked.

"Nothing," Chloe said, but she knew that she was lying. She had a hunch the farmhouse held a lot of secrets. She only hoped she would have a chance to glimpse a few of them before the police ordered her off the property. "Nothing at all."

Lex Luthor resisted the urge to slam down the phone. Instead, he put the receiver gently in its cradle, then he stood and shoved his hands in his pockets.

Good thing he was alone in his study. He felt like yelling at someone, anyone, for any reason he could think of. He pushed his leather chair back, then walked to the window and gazed out at the garden.

Anyone who saw him would think he was calm. Lex had become good at looking calm, especially when he was angry. And right now, he was furious.

For three days, his father had been refusing to talk with him, always putting him off whenever Lex managed to reach him.

I told you that you were in charge of the Smallville LuthorCorp plant, Lex, his father would say. *That means the good and the bad.*

But Lex wasn't calling about LuthorCorp—not exactly, anyway. He wasn't even calling to ask advice. He wanted to let his father know about the growing unrest in Smallville.

Even though Lex's father claimed Lex was in charge of the LuthorCorp plant, his father still made the final decisions. And the layoffs that his father had ordered three months before were causing Lex great headaches.

Lex wanted his father to come to Smallville to see the trouble the layoffs had caused.

Somehow, his father seemed to know that, and was dodging Lex at every turn. And this afternoon was the worst. This afternoon, Lex's father wasn't even answering his cell phone when Lex called.

Lex would have to find a number that wasn't in his father's caller I.D., and try again. Then his father would have to pick up.

Lex leaned his head against the window. The glass was hot against his forehead, and he pulled back. He had forgotten the heat wave outside. The air-conditioning inside the mansion kept everything at a constant sixty-eight degrees year-round, just the way he liked it.

But outside the plants seemed to be struggling. The tulips he'd had specially imported from Holland were wilting, their colors almost bleeding into the ground. Even the trees, which had just started to leaf in the last few days, seemed exhausted.

If he hadn't seen the weather on a local station at lunch, he would have thought some strange Smallville anomaly was happening again. But this unseasonably warm weather stretched from New York to Denver. Kansans were suffering just like three-quarters of the nation.

Small consolation. Just as it was a small consolation that his father rarely answered anyone's calls. Until this afternoon, he took his son's even if they were fighting, which they usually were.

Lex turned back to his desk and sighed. The phone sat in the middle of the blotter, taunting him. He should call his father's secretary back and force her to put him through. She wouldn't be able to give Lex the same excuse twice, and if she tried, Lex would throw it in her face.

His father wasn't incommunicado. If there was anything Lex Luthor knew about his father, it was that Lionel Luthor was never incommunicado. The people who needed to get through to him did.

Apparently, Lionel Luthor no longer considered his son one of those people.

Lex shook his head. He should have known it was coming. He and his father had never been on good terms.

Lex moved the phone off the blotter, away from the center of the desk. He would handle the situation in Smallville himself. He had planned to anyway. He had just wanted his father to see how bad it had gotten.

But his father never liked to face the dark side of his policies—not for any reason, not for anyone.

Lex had no idea why he had deluded himself into thinking he had more influence with his father than anyone else did. After all these years, and all the times his father had proved to Lex just how little he mattered, it was amazing how badly his father's snubs still hurt.

Clark's hand felt like it was covered in slime. His clothes clung wetly to him, and his shoes sloshed as he walked.

He was trying not to think about how Danny Franklin's hand had felt in his own, how the skin had slipped over the bone as Clark tugged the body toward the edge of the pond.

Still, when he, Lana, and Chloe reached the first barn, he had to stop at the pump and rinse off his hands. Neither Chloe nor Lana said anything to him as he rubbed cold water over his fingers. He would have expected Chloe to mention the whole crime scene thing again, but she didn't.

Instead, she gave him a sympathetic look before she turned away, as if she were glad it was him instead of her who had fished Danny Franklin's body out of that pond.

Lana, on the other hand, stared at Clark but didn't seem to see him. He had a hunch she was in shock, and he wasn't sure what to do about it.

He wasn't exactly feeling great himself. He'd liked Danny Franklin. They hadn't been close friends, but they'd known each other for years. Sometimes they banded together—two of the only guys in Smallville whose chores prevented them from going out for the football team, even though that wasn't precisely true for Clark.

He didn't go out because his parents felt he would forget, and use his abilities to unfair advantage. And the one time he had the opportunity to be on the team, that had happened.

"I think we should spread out," Chloe was saying to Lana. "See if we can find anything."

Clark shook his head ever so slightly. Chloe was as shocked as he and Lana had been, but after a second in which Clark thought Chloe was going to lose her lunch, she gathered herself and went into reporter mode.

It didn't mean she was coping any better than Lana was. In fact, there were times when Clark thought this method—the I-Must-Have-As-Much-Information-As-Possible-Right-Now method—was even more dangerous than being numb. Chloe had a history of opening the wrong door, getting into the wrong situation, finding the wrong thing at the wrong time.

"Spread out?" Lana repeated, but she didn't seem to be listening. She was still clutching her cell phone in her right hand and was looking behind her at the pond.

"I don't think that's a good idea, Chloe," Clark said, splashing cold water on his face. That felt good. Maybe he had gotten hotter than he realized. "I think we need to stick together."

"You don't think whoever killed Danny is still here, do you?" Chloe asked.

"Killed Danny?" Lana blinked. The phrase seemed to bring her out of her shock. "I thought he drowned."

"We don't know," Clark said. "He looks like he drowned, but Chloe reminded me earlier that his death was not a natural one, so the police will deal with this like a crime scene."

There was a slight furrow in Lana's forehead.

"That doesn't mean," Clark added hastily, "that Danny was murdered. Just that his death is unusual."

"To say the least." Chloe shifted from foot to foot. "You done bathing now, Clark? Can we look around? I don't think we have a lot of time left."

And, he thought, there was that edge in her voice, the one she got when she was feeling overwhelmed, but didn't want to admit it—even to herself.

"Let's go." Clark let go of the pump and deliberately

walked past Chloe. He was going to lead this search, and if he saw something he didn't like, he would stop it immediately.

"I think we should check the house first," Lana said. "Just like we planned. Maybe they're out searching for Danny. Maybe they don't realize . . ."

Her voice trailed off and she looked down. Clark put a reassuring hand on her shoulder, squeezed, and let go quickly. His wet fingers left a moist handprint on her shirt.

He didn't say as he passed her—he didn't dare—that if Danny Franklin had been missing, and his parents had been worried enough to look for him, then the entire school would have known about it. All of Smallville would have.

Because Smallville had such a bizarre history of strange goings-on, the police were pretty vocal in the first days of a search for a missing person. And there had been no notices in the paper, no flyers posted, no announcements in home room or at school.

In fact, no one seemed too concerned about Danny's absence, except Lana. She'd spoken up about it long before their assignment was due. But the only way she'd been able to get anyone to take her seriously—Clark included—had been to mention the lab work.

He sighed and took long steps to catch up to Chloe.

"Did he have bruises on his head?" she asked. "You know, the kind of thing that would have happened if he bumped his head and then fell into the water."

Danny's face had been chalk white, with blue lines through it. Even his eyelids had been blue.

And that was odd, now that Clark considered it. Danny's eyes were closed.

Clark had never seen a drowning victim before, but he had a hunch that none of them died with their eyes closed.

"I didn't look that closely, Chloe," Clark said as carefully as he could.

He crossed the yard to the sidewalk. Weeds grew between cracks in the concrete. Up close, the detail work he had so admired seemed like work from a previous season. Between the daffodils and tulips were dead twigs, leaves, and the brown hulks of last fall's plants.

No one had cleaned up the flower beds when the snow melted. He doubted anyone had mowed the lawn either, although it was too hard to tell this early in the year.

The front porch floor was covered with winter dirt, and more leaves, piled in a corner. If he had left the fall leaves like that, his father would go after him. Leaves made good composting, and should have been in the compost pile long before winter set in.

"I would have expected this place to be a lot neater," Chloe said.

Lana was staring at the leaves, too. "It used to be. It used to be perfect. It would drive me crazy. Nell likes a clean house, but Danny's mother used to make their house perfect—and with three kids on top of it."

Clark gave Lana a sideways look. He hadn't realized she'd been to Danny's house before. Lana didn't notice his gaze, but Chloe did. She rolled her eyes like she always did when she thought Clark was mooning over Lana.

"Well, with a wraparound porch like that," Chloe said, sounding businesslike, "we should be able to see inside. I just need to look through that picture window and maybe get a few shots."

"I don't think that's a good idea, Chloe," Clark said. "After all, you don't know what you'll find."

And neither did he. He should have planned for this. He stopped on the sidewalk and made himself scan the farmhouse for bodies. He concentrated, and his special vision activated.

His vision passed through the walls into the main rooms proper. He didn't see anyone—alive or dead.

"I'm not suggesting we go in, Clark." Chloe started up the stairs, almost stomping in her impatience. "I just have a feeling that we might find something else here."

Clark had that sense too, but unlike Chloe, the idea of finding something else didn't attract him. He hurried to the steps and accompanied her up.

Lana followed, wiping her finger against the rail as if its dirt surprised her as well.

Chloe walked over to the picture window and pressed her face against the glass. Clark came up beside her and looked.

He didn't need his special vision to know that Chloe's hunch had been right. The couch was overturned, an end table was smashed against the wall, and a throw rug was bunched in the middle of the room. Other furniture had been flung aside, as if it had been in the way of something—or someone.

Lana stopped beside him. Chloe already had her camera out and was taking pictures.

Clark was glad Chloe was respecting the crime scene. That meant that as much as she wanted to, she wouldn't go inside.

"Do you think I'd contaminate anything if I just walked into each room, taking pictures?" Chloe asked as if she could read Clark's mind.

"Yes," he said.

Chloe frowned at the house as if it were the problem. "Maybe I'll just wander around the outside—"

"No, Chloe," Clark said.

Lana hadn't moved from the window. "The house never looked like this. If Mrs. Franklin were here, she'd clean it up, no matter what happened."

"I think it's pretty clear that they're not here," Chloe said.

"Or inside," Lana said. It was obvious what she was thinking. She was thinking there were more bodies in the house.

Clark didn't know how to tell her that he knew there weren't. It would be false reassurance anyway.

He had no idea what had happened to the Franklin family, but judging from the evidence, he knew it couldn't have been good.

CHAPTER FOUR

Lionel Luthor's shoulders ached. Perhaps "ached" wasn't the correct word. Perhaps "tugged" was. He'd had this feeling in his shoulders before, when he'd hung by his arms from the bar in his private gym, holding his entire weight off the ground.

But his hands weren't holding anything. They were behind him, their backs resting against the silk of his suit. His wrists were crossed and sore.

And he was tired. Very tired.

Nauseous, too. A swimming sort of nausea, the kind induced by too much drink (something he hadn't indulged in for decades) combined with movement.

Movement. Like a car, turning a corner too fast. And then another corner, and another, bump along a poorly paved road, hitting potholes, making his face bounce against the leather car seat.

Face, bouncing. Drool on the side of his mouth. Mouth dry, as if he hadn't had water for days.

His feet were asleep, his knees bent. He was on his side—and he was tied up.

His eyelids flickered, but he didn't open his eyes. He remembered—just in time—the crowd, the heat, the bank. The way his security people had gone down. His limo driver—his favorite employee—toppling over like a statue in the hands of a careless art patron.

The air-conditioning was on high. He was shivering now, where before he had been too hot. Maybe it was the effect of the drug that had knocked him out.

The car turned again, left this time, judging by the way he

slid on the seat, and the nausea rose. He moaned before he had even realized he made the sound—no way to block it now. He just had to accept that he had let that one slip, and be vigilant. Ever vigilant.

"Hey, boss."

Bad old movie word, "boss." It needed to be spoken with a Jersey accent—or a Joisey accent to be more accurate. But this voice was calm, with a touch of Kansas—the prairies, not Metropolis.

Luthor kept his eyes closed, careful not to squeeze them shut. Still, his eyelashes fluttered. What had been in that drug? He didn't have complete control over his body—at least, not like he was used to.

"I think he's coming out of it."

"Give him some more." This voice was different, deeper. Another Kansas accent, prairie, not city, and something about the way the words flowed made Luthor think that "Boss" had less of an education than the first speaker, not more.

"More? Won't that hurt him?"

A third voice, also male. Same accent.

He didn't remember seeing a third player, but it made sense. It would have taken a lot of people to bring down his security team.

"What do you care?" Boss again.

"We don't want to hurt him," Third Voice said.

"We don't want to *kill* him," Boss said. "I don't care if he gets hurt along the way."

Luthor tried to remain motionless so that they'd continue to think he was out. He couldn't test the strength of his bonds because he wasn't sure how they were watching him. The limo had security cameras everywhere.

He had had them installed so that he could watch the driver or, if he chose to, he could sit in the front seat and see whatever happened in the back. If they were watching him from the front, they could see his every movement.

"A second dose won't kill him," Boss said. "Besides, we gave him less than his employees. They didn't die. Give him another dose, and he'll be no worse off than they are."

"How do we know they didn't die?" Third Voice asked. "We left them behind."

Luthor liked that piece of information. Their bodies alongside the road made the circumstances of his disappearance fairly obvious.

And when the most powerful man in Metropolis had been kidnapped, the police would scramble into action quickly. They'd have to call in the FBI, who always played well with Luthor's security team.

He'd get out of this, if he could keep himself alive.

"If we'd wanted to kill them, we would have killed them," Boss said. "Now shut up."

Maybe he could bargain with these men. They clearly wanted something from one of his companies—or maybe from him. If all they needed was money, he could provide that, and use it to catch them later. It would take very little, and he could be persuasive when he needed to be.

He had to start talking before they dosed him again.

He opened his eyes in time to see a small plant mister, held in a gloved hand, approach his nose. He looked up, saw an alien with a hose instead of a mouth, clear square eyes, a green face.

The gloved fingers squeezed the mister's trigger before Luthor could protest. He had his mouth half-open as the spray hit his face. Some of it landed on his tongue, filling his mouth with the rancid taste of spoiled orange soda pop.

As his consciousness started to drift again, he realized he wasn't looking at an alien at all. He was looking at a man wearing a military-issue gas mask. A man who was afraid the spray would get on him.

His dizziness increased, and he fought, just like he had the first time, even though he knew he'd lose.

Mist. They'd sprayed him in the crowd. And his security team. Had the kidnappers been wearing masks then? Probably. They'd kept their heads down. Which meant that not only Luthor's people had been knocked out. Others. . . .

The thought trailed out of his head. He tumbled into blackness so deep he could no longer feel anything.

Not even himself.

The ambulance arrived first, its lights and sirens off. The drivers barreled down the gravel driveway as if it were an interstate. A sheriff's car followed right behind, its red-and-blue lights flashing.

Apparently, the locked gate at the end of the driveway hadn't bothered any of the authorities. Had they gone around it? Or had they figured out a way to open it?

Clark didn't know. He stepped away from the road, pulling Lana and Chloe back with him. Lana's face still didn't have enough color. Chloe had run out of room on her digital camera, and had been mumbling something about downloading to her laptop when the ambulance finally showed up.

"Why do they bring in an ambulance when someone's dead?" Lana asked.

"I don't know," Clark said. "They just do."

"Because they never know what they're going to find," Chloe said as if she knew. Maybe she did. "Sometimes people who seem dead aren't."

Lana looked over her shoulder at Danny's body. Clark couldn't help himself; he looked, too.

Danny was still sprawled facedown in the weeds, right where Clark had left him.

One of the paramedics got out of the ambulance. "Where?" he said to Clark, Chloe, and Lana.

"Over there." Clark nodded toward Danny's body.

The paramedics hurried down the slight incline toward the pond. When they reached Danny, they crouched.

Lana looked away.

"You kids the ones who called?" A Lowell County deputy that Clark did not recognize walked down the driveway toward them. Another deputy, also in plain clothes, joined the paramedics.

In the distance, sirens wailed. They were on the main highway and getting closer.

"I called," Lana said. She sounded stronger than Clark had expected her to.

"So you three found him?" The deputy looked suspicious.

"Clark did," Lana said. Apparently she hadn't heard the same suspicion in his tone that Clark had.

"You?" the deputy asked Clark.

Clark nodded.

"What made you go into the water? Skinny-dipping?"

Chloe's face flamed. "Of course not." She answered even though the question was meant for Clark. "We were down here looking for Danny."

"And you found him." The deputy's eyebrows went up, as if he thought the whole thing a miracle. "How amazing is that?"

Lana frowned. "It's not amazing at all. He was floating—"

"I saw him first," Chloe said over her. "Clark just pulled him out."

"It was—"

"Roberts!" The other deputy waved his arm from below. "Come see this."

"You kids stay right here," the deputy, who was apparently named Roberts, said. Then he trudged toward the side of the pond.

"As if we're going anywhere," Lana said under her breath. She had snapped out of shock and had clearly moved into annoyed. Not that Clark could blame her. That cop had an attitude, and he obviously didn't trust them.

The other sirens had grown a lot closer.

Chloe was watching the paramedics and the deputies. Her arms were folded over her camera strap. "They don't even seem to care if they're trampling the evidence."

"There's no way he could be alive, is there, Clark?" Lana asked softly.

Clark shook his head. No living person was ever that cold and rubbery feeling. Not to mention the way the skin had slid under his hand.

Clark shuddered, in spite of himself.

"Then what do you think they're doing?" Lana asked.

Chloe frowned. She took a step forward and squinted. "I think they might have found something else."

"What?" Lana asked.

But Clark knew. He had felt something brush against his leg as he stepped into the shallow water. Something cold and slimy, that touched him ever so lightly. Like fingers, tapping against his ankle.

He hadn't thought to look for another body. He had been so surprised to find Danny's. Clark had gotten Danny to shore, and then had planned to turn around, to look in the water for the cause of that frightening little touch, but Chloe had stopped him.

Chloe with her talk of crime scenes and contamination.

And murder.

Clark glanced at the house. Lana had said that Mrs. Franklin wouldn't leave it like that.

The car was missing, but Danny was here.

The barn door was closed, and the gate was locked.

Someone—or several someones—didn't want anyone to come to the Franklin farm. They had made it as uninviting as possible.

"What is it, Clark?" Chloe asked.

The sirens were very close now, so close they hurt his ears. He had sensitive hearing, too, always had, but it seemed even more sensitive at the moment. Chloe and Lana didn't seem to notice how loud the sirens had become.

He looked away from the house, back at the pond.

The paramedics were pointing at the water's edge.

Two more police cars jolted down the driveway, pulling to a stop in a haze of dust. The sirens shut off, but the lights continued to turn.

"Clark?" Chloe asked again.

"Put your camera away, Chloe," Clark said. He had to distract her, at least for a moment, so that he could check out his hunch.

"It's useless, Clark. I'm not getting rid of the pictures I have, and I'm out of memory. If I—"

"Put it away, Chloe," he said again, "or the police might confiscate it for evidence."

"They wouldn't. I'm a member of the press." Chloe said.

"I don't think the *Torch* commands as much respect as the *Daily Planet*," Lana said. "At best, you'd have a fight on your hands."

"I hate it when you're right," Chloe said, and bent over to pick up her book bag.

Clark focused on the water. He used his X-ray vision, boring through the murk. A lot of sand and silt, still stirred up from his trip through the filthy water. Sunlight filtered through, though, changing one area from black-brown to a light tan.

A hand bobbed gently against the muddy bottom.

Clark scanned the pond. The muddy water was hard to see through, but he could see enough.

The body near the edge was long and thin, hair floating upward, concealing the face. But the hand was a giveaway. The fake rhinestone-studded fingernails and rings on every finger.

He remembered how those fingernails had felt, scraping his scalp, when those fingers ruffled his hair just a week ago, the scent of bubble gum and vanilla perfume overwhelming him.

Wow, Danny, you didn't tell me how Clark had turned out, Betty Franklin had said. Betty was—had been—Danny's flirtatious older sister. Her identical twin sister, Bonnie, had given Clark a sympathetic smile that day, almost as if she had been apologizing for Betty.

Bonnie had never been as flamboyant as her twin, but the two of them were rarely apart.

Only they were now. Apart forever. Because Bonnie wasn't in that pond. No one else was. Just Betty.

"What's the matter, Clark?" Lana asked.

He swallowed, not sure how to answer.

Then the paramedics answered for him. "We got another one!"

And every person in the area burst into action.

CHAPTER FIVE

The cops ran down the side of the hill, trampling weeds, and leaving footprints in the mud. A group of men had gathered along the water's edge, two of them—the paramedics?—wading in, and grabbing at something.

Chloe hurried down the driveway, stepping off the gravel in the same place the cops had. She had trampled innocently before. If she was going to contaminate a crime scene this time, she was going to do it the way the cops had.

Her fingers itched for her camera, but she knew better than to haul it out. Clark's warning had been a good one; the cops would confiscate her camera, and anything else she brought out, maybe even her notebook.

She would have to memorize everything. And she could do it. She'd done it before. What it took was simple: she had to write up her notes the moment she got back to the *Torch*'s office.

When she did that, she'd have a story good enough to get picked up by the local paper, maybe even good enough to sell to the *Planet*.

Clark was calling after her. He probably didn't want her down here. He was so protective, and so sweet, even if he didn't seem to share the crush she had for him.

But she wasn't going to listen to him. She had to be able to see what was going on.

The men thrashed in the water, creating waves. There was no smell this time, beyond that of stagnant water and algae. There was also no conversation. Everyone seemed to be working in complete silence, as if this were a routine that they'd all gone through before.

The paramedics were reaching into the water, pulling at something. An arm flopped out. Chloe could only see the elbow and the biceps, elegant and thin, unnaturally white. She finally understood what all those Victorian novels she read in English meant when they used the word "alabaster" to describe skin.

Although she suspected they didn't mean that the person with alabaster skin was dead.

Chloe felt light-headed, but she made herself take a deep breath. Professional reporter. Professional. Calm in a crisis. Noting the details.

No one had noticed her standing there yet, but it would only be a matter of time.

Two of the cops got behind the body and lifted it by the ankles. Water drained off the blue jeans and the sweater that covered the torso.

Long hair—dark, Chloe couldn't tell what color exactly—plastered against the face, hiding it. The body was female; that much was clear, but Chloe couldn't tell whose it was.

Until the arm flopped again, the hand trailing toward the water as if reaching for something in the murky depths. Rings on every finger, including a large fake turquoise one on the thumb.

Only one girl in school wore a turquoise ring on her thumb, and she was a senior. Flirtatious, difficult, extremely pretty. Danny Franklin used to shake his head as his sister Betty went by, saying she'd get them all in trouble.

Chloe used to think that was just an expression. Now she wondered if it meant something else.

"I don't think you should get any closer."

It was Clark, standing just behind her. Chloe hadn't even heard him come up, and she always noticed what Clark was doing. Always.

"I wasn't planning to go closer," she said, keeping her

voice down. She wanted to be as unobtrusive as possible for as long as possible. "It's Betty Franklin, you know."

"I know," Clark said quietly.

"Oh . . ." Apparently Lana had joined them too. Chloe hadn't heard her either.

Chloe gave her a sideways look. Lana had a hand over her mouth. "Were you friends with Betty, too?"

Lana shook her head. "She was a senior, and way too popular to have time for someone like me."

Someone like Lana Lang, the most popular girl in their class? Get real. Chloe normally would have said that, but this wasn't normal at all.

The men carried the body out of the pond. The water sloshed and moved, looking like a live thing.

Enough strange things happened in Smallville that the thought wasn't as odd as it seemed. Chloe resisted the urge to take a step back. She wasn't close enough to the water to have it touch her.

"Clark, you don't think that the water . . . ?" Chloe let her voice trail off, feeling like what she had been about to ask wasn't appropriate. Somehow, having a discussion better fit for the *Weekly World News* while the police took bodies of people she knew out of a pond didn't seem right.

But Clark was looking at her, those blue eyes intense. "The water what?"

Chloe shrugged, pretending a nonchalance she didn't feel. "Nothing."

"Do you think this is something for your wall of weird?" Lana asked. There was sadness in her voice, which surprised Chloe. Somehow she had expected anger. Lana hated the fact that Chloe put details of all the strange things that happened around Smallville on a wall in the *Torch* office. Since Lana's parents had been killed by the meteor storm that Chloe figured started all the weirdness, Lana found the wall insulting. After all, she was a centerpiece on it, her three-year-old face on a magazine cover the picture of grief.

"It just seems so surreal," Chloe said, deciding not to answer the question.

"It's only going to get worse," Clark said.

"What do you mean?" Lana asked the question so softly that Chloe barely heard her.

Clark got that worried weight-of-the-world look on his face. "Betty never went anywhere without Bonnie. And you're the one who mentioned that Danny's mom wouldn't have left the house like that."

"I did, didn't I?" Lana's mouth thinned.

Chloe felt a fluttering in her stomach. Nerves. It had to be nerves.

The paramedics set Betty down beside Danny.

"And no one leaves a farm like this, not in the spring, not a farmer who cares as much as Danny's dad." Clark was watching the cops, too. They were combing the pond as best they could without divers.

But Clark had already checked the pond. He knew that no more bodies rested in it.

"Do you think they're all dead?" Chloe asked.

Clark's gaze met hers. She was startled by the intensity in his eyes. "What do you think?" he asked.

"I think one dead teenager in a pond is probably a tragic accident. Two is probably something else, something deliberate." Chloe hadn't really realized she'd been having those thoughts until Clark dragged them out of her.

"That's my sense of it, too," Clark said.

"I can't believe the whole family is dead." Lana's voice rose.

Chloe shushed her, but the damage was done. The cop, the one who had been so unfriendly, waded out of the water and gestured at them.

"You kids," he said. "Back away from here. There's no more to see."

Clark put his hand on Chloe's shoulder just as she had been about to argue. "Let's go," he said quietly.

Another cop walked toward them. Chloe didn't move, even though Clark was trying to get her to.

"We have every right to be here," Chloe said. "We're—"

"The ones who found the first body, I know," the deputy said. He was younger than the other one, and familiar-looking. Chloe had seen him around town a lot since she'd taken over the *Torch*. He was one of the younger officers, and one of the nicer ones. "We'll need some statements from each of you, so you'll have to hang around, but Roberts is right. You don't need to see any more of this."

"Do you think there are more bodies?" Chloe asked.

The cop gave her a measuring look. Then recognition filled his gaze. "You're the girl who runs the *Torch*, right?"

"I'm the *person* in charge," Chloe said, trying not to bristle at the word "girl."

"Well, I can't give you quotes. Obviously, this is an investigation now."

"But you think you're going to find something else, don't you?" Lana asked. She had a way of making the question sound innocent, where Chloe always made questions sound like an interrogation. Chloe wished she could learn that trick from Lana.

"Let's just say there's a possibility," the cop said. He held out his arms, as if he were trying to physically protect the crime scene. "I'm going to walk you guys to the gate. Someone'll be there shortly to take your statements."

"We can just wait up by the house," Chloe said.

The cop shook his head. "There's already been enough activity around this spot. Let us do our job. When we're done, you can do yours."

Chloe sighed, but she knew he was right. And the time he was going to give her at the gate would give her a chance to make some notes about everything she saw.

"I like the Franklins," Lana said as the three of them walked up the driveway to the gate. "Why did something like this have to happen to them?"

Why indeed? Chloe didn't answer and neither did Clark. There was nothing either of them could say.

Smallville was cursed. Chloe knew that better than anyone else in town. But knowing that didn't make living through days like this any easier.

Lex got the news through his e-mail. He had his e-mail program set up to alert him whenever there was breaking news that might affect the stocks he was watching.

The e-mail program pinged just as Lex was about to leave the study to go to his fencing lesson. He had planned to be particularly aggressive that afternoon, to work off some of the anger his father had provoked.

Lex almost didn't go back and check the alert. But he had done that in the past and had missed some great buy opportunities on stocks that were going through an "adjustment."

He walked back to the desk. The alert icon was flashing in the top right of his screen. He tapped the mouse, opening the e-mail.

LUTHORCORP STOCK PLUMMETS

His breath caught. He'd checked the stock thirty minutes ago. It was fine.

He made himself concentrate on the article.

. . . LuthorCorp stock suddenly finds itself subject to heavy trading as analysts try to digest this afternoon's late-breaking news involving LuthorCorp's founder Lionel Luthor. Luthor's security guards and driver were found unconscious outside City Bank, along with bystanders, all of whom collapsed on the street.

Initially, authorities believed the mass fainting had been due to some kind of reaction to the terrible heat, but within the last fifteen minutes, it has become clear that the attack on Luthor's people was deliberate.

Lionel Luthor, last seen outside the bank, is missing, and so is one of the company's limousines, a black stretch model with the vanity plate LUTHOR 1. . . .

Lex wasn't breathing. He made himself exhale and then inhale, his breath suddenly rapid. No one had called him. The entire staff of LuthorCorp—hell, probably the entire population of Kansas—knew that his father had been kidnapped, and no one bothered to let him know.

Lex's fists clenched. He stood, then froze.

Was this a ploy? His father wouldn't want the stock to plummet like that, but the Luthors—both Lionel and Lex—had enemies who would. Not to mention LuthorCorp itself. People hated its success, and always tried to destroy it from the outside.

Lex whirled, grabbed the phone off its cradle and dialed his father's cell.

It rang, and finally, the voice mail picked up. Just like before.

Lex's stomach tightened.

The secondary line rang, and Lex grabbed it. "What?"

"Mr. Luthor?"

Lex didn't recognize the voice, but that didn't mean anything. His father often went through assistants so fast that Lex couldn't keep up.

"This is Lex Luthor."

"I'm John Harrison. I'm one of the deputy security chiefs for your father's company."

A deputy chief low enough on the pay scale that he got the job of calling Luthor's recalcitrant son to give him the bad news. A few years ago, Lex might even have made that comment.

He had learned control since then. He wasn't going to let on that he knew anything. Not yet, anyway.

"Yes?" he said, keeping his voice flat, disinterested.

"Um, have you heard the news, Mr. Luthor?"

"I don't know, Mr. Harrison. What news should I have heard?"

"Um, about your father."

"My father's always in the news, Mr. Harrison. I really don't pay a lot of attention. Unless there's something going on that I haven't been informed about?" Lex added just enough of an inflection on that last so that a smart person might realize that Lex knew more than he was letting on.

"Your father, sir." Harrison's voice was shaking. "We have reason to believe he was kidnapped."

So it was true. Lex gripped the receiver so tightly that his hand hurt. "Reason to believe?"

"Yes, sir. We haven't had any confirmation yet, but—"

"What sort of confirmation do you need?" Lex asked. "Either he was kidnapped or he wasn't."

"What I mean is that no one has called with a ransom demand yet."

"So you don't know if he's been kidnapped or murdered." Lex's fingernails bit into the receiver. He could feel the hard plastic dig into the soft skin of his fingertips.

"Well, sir, I wouldn't put it that way, sir. I mean, the bodyguards are all right—"

"Really?" Lex let some of the anger he was feeling out. "Then they weren't doing their job, were they? They were supposed to protect my father, with their lives if need be."

"Yes, sir. But—"

"But?" Lex stood. "What else can you give me? Hmmm? My stupid e-mail stock updates gave me more than you have. My father was taken off a busy Metropolis street in broad daylight. Several guards and bystanders are down. My father was taken in his own car. What have you people done since you got the news? You certainly hadn't contacted me. I assume that was because you were too busy."

"We were trying to confirm—"

"Trying to confirm that something happened? While my father could be dying? Don't you know the first few hours are crucial? Get to it, man. Make sure the Metropolis police—ah, hell. I'll do it myself."

Lex slammed the receiver down so hard, the phone cradle shattered. He didn't care what he ruined. He was too angry. These security people were utter failures. They were just sheep waiting for someone to tell them what to do. Without a strong leader, they had no idea how to proceed.

Idiots. They were letting his father die.

Lex froze then. His father, dead. How often had he wished for that? Almost every day at the first boarding school. A little less as time went on.

And sometimes, Lex had no idea what he would do without his father, without that constant struggle for acceptance, without someone strong to push against.

His father kidnapped. Maybe dead.

Lionel Luthor, gone.

It wasn't possible. His father was indestructible. Or so it

usually seemed to Lex. Even though that wasn't true. His father was just as human as the rest of them.

Just as vulnerable.

He could die, just like everyone else.

Unless someone competent did something. Unless Lex stepped in.

He reached over the desk, punched the computer, turning off the screensaver, and then shut the computer down. He grabbed his cell phone and the keys to his Porsche.

By the time he was across the room, he was on the phone with LuthorCorp's private jet service. He was clear about what he needed: when he reached Smallville's tiny airport, he wanted a corporate jet fueled up and ready to take off.

He wanted to be in Metropolis within the hour. Because, thanks to imbeciles like Harrison, there wasn't time to waste.

CHAPTER SIX

"What an awful tragedy." Clark's mother put both of her hands on his shoulders, and leaned against him, pressing her cheek against the top of his head. "I can't imagine what it would be like to lose one child, let alone two."

The kitchen table was piled with food. His father had hauled the grill out of the garage, a spring ritual that they hadn't gotten to do earlier this year. The chicken smelled terrific, and Clark's mom had finished off the meal with baked beans, potato salad, and corn bread she had made the day before.

Usually a spread like this would have cheered Clark up. But the day's events disturbed him. He kept feeling like he had missed something. If he had only known something was wrong sooner, he might have been able to save them.

Of course, he didn't say anything like that to his parents. They'd had this conversation many times. His parents would tell him he wasn't responsible for other people's actions and that sometimes, no matter how many abilities he had, he wouldn't be able to stop bad things from happening.

Clark knew deep down that his parents were right, but that didn't change how he felt. Sometimes he wondered what all his miraculous powers were for if he couldn't help people he cared about.

His father took a barbecued chicken leg off the platter in the center of the table. He glanced at Clark—a warning look of some kind that Clark didn't entirely understand. Something about his mother and the way she worried, but his dad always worried about that.

"We don't know what happened up there, Martha," his dad said. "The police aren't saying."

"Well, we know what Clark told us." His mom squeezed Clark's shoulders, then moved away from him, grabbing a plate of day-old corn bread off the kitchen counter. "At least two of the Franklin children are gone. Who knows what's happened to everyone else?"

"The farm looked pretty deserted." Clark grabbed the stoneware pot filled with baked beans. An hour ago, he would have thought he couldn't have eaten anything. But his stomach was rumbling just like it usually did.

If only he didn't think about Danny and Betty Franklin.

"But the fields were tilled?" his dad asked for the second time.

"Tilled but no fertilizer. It was like everything stopped last week," Clark said.

"If a body'd been in the water more than a week, then—"

"Enough," his mom said as she sat down. She put the corn bread on the table near the potato salad. "We're having dinner."

Usually Clark hated it when she limited dinnertime talk, but he was grateful tonight. He didn't want to think about bodies any more than he had to.

"All I was saying, Martha, is that it sounds like the work stopped before the tragedy. Tragedies." His dad took the baked beans from Clark's hand. "This is the wrong time of year to stop work on a farm, no matter what's going on."

Clark's mom used tongs to take a thigh off the platter. "What do you think happened?"

"I don't know," his dad said. "If the house was as messed up as Clark said, then maybe some stranger came in and tried to rob them."

"Killing Betty and Danny?" his mom asked. "What about the rest of the family?"

"We were trying to figure that out." Clark took a chicken breast and a piece of corn bread. He couldn't quite face the potato salad. The eggs made him uncomfortable in a way he didn't want to examine. "I used my special vision to look in the house and I didn't see anyone. Before we left, I checked the two barns, too. There was nothing."

"Was there anything strange about the water, Clark?" his mother asked.

"Not that I could see." Clark took a bite of chicken. It was good. He had forgotten how much he liked the first grilled meal of the season.

"No nearby meteor rocks?"

"No," Clark said. "And I was close enough to notice."

"We're awful proud of you, son," his dad said. "The way you went right into that water."

"I'd feel better if I could have found Danny before he drowned," Clark said.

"I thought the police weren't sure how he died." His mom stopped buttering her corn bread. She studied him, holding the butter knife upward as if it were a weapon.

"They aren't," Clark said. "I guess I'm just hoping it's something innocent. You know. Some kind of accident."

"I think we can guarantee that it's not something innocent," his dad said. "Two people don't just die like that, not around here, and not in ponds that shallow, especially when there aren't roads nearby."

"You don't think they were drunk and fell in?" Clark's mom asked.

"Danny didn't drink," Clark said. "He was a good guy."

"Everyone makes mistakes sometimes, Clark," his mom said.

"And we don't always know people as well as we think we do." His dad finished the chicken leg and reached for another.

"I know, Dad," Clark said. "But drinking's not something kids hide, at least from other kids. Danny didn't do that. I don't know about Betty. She ran with a different crowd. But Danny, he was a lot more interested in grades and school and stuff than hanging out with the drinkers on Friday night."

"I don't think he would have had time for that anyway," Clark's mom said. "A lot of the farming chores fell to him when his dad went to work. And Danny didn't have Clark's abilities."

"I know." Clark's father sighed. "The problem is, Martha, crimes are usually pretty logical things. Two dead kids and a trashed-up house doesn't bode well for the missing family members."

"The car's missing, too," Clark said.

"Yeah, and anyone could have taken it after killing the Franklins and messing up the house. I'm sure the police are looking into that angle."

Clark's mom put her napkin alongside her plate. "I would think it would be difficult to murder an entire family, Jonathan, particularly since all five of them were full-grown."

"You're thinking of only one killer," Clark's dad said.

"A gang of killers?" Clark asked. "Isn't that a bit far-fetched for Smallville?"

"This place isn't as innocent or safe as we'd like it to be, Clark," his dad said. "The whole country has changed in that way."

"Still," his mom said, "you'd think someone would have escaped, and gotten help."

Clark hadn't even thought of that. He had done his best that afternoon, but he had been as shaky as Lana and Chloe. It was hard to look into the face of a dead friend.

"There's a lot of woods around there," his mom was saying. "Someone who knew the area could hide out for days."

"Without getting help?" his dad asked. "I'd think by now we would have known."

"The weather hasn't been that good until today, Jonathan. And if the person was injured, there might be a possibility that they're still out there."

"Maybe I should look," Clark said. "I should have done it when we were there before. Chloe wanted to, but I didn't think it was safe."

"You had the right instincts, Clark," his dad said. "Besides, I'm pretty sure the authorities have already thought of this. They've probably searched the woods."

"But they don't have the advantage I do," Clark said. "I can see things no one else can."

"I don't think that would be a good idea, Clark." His dad pushed his plate back. "Let the authorities handle this one."

Clark's mom frowned. "You're not saying everything you're thinking, Jonathan."

His dad pushed his plate away. "I don't like what I'm thinking."

Clark took a sip of milk. It was cold and fresh. It tasted good. "What do you mean, Dad?"

His dad shook his head.

"You brought it up," Clark's mom said. "You may as well finish. We'll be wondering otherwise."

"Jed Franklin's been under a lot of pressure, that's all. And sometimes people under a lot of pressure do strange things." Clark's dad pushed his chair away from the table. He picked up his plate and carried it to the sink.

"You don't think—?"

"I'm sure I'm not the only one considering it, Martha," his dad said. "You mentioned yourself how difficult you thought it would be to kill an entire family."

Clark's mom shook her head. "I never thought Jed Franklin could hurt anyone. He seemed like such a gentle man."

"Push a man to the edge, and he might just fall off," Clark's dad said. "Jed Franklin has been on that edge for years. The last time I saw him, he was saying some mighty nasty things about LuthorCorp, things I never expected to come from Jed Franklin's mouth."

"It's a long way from hating LuthorCorp to killing your family," Clark's mom said.

"Besides, you'd have to be crazy to do that," Clark added.

They all stared at each other for a moment. His dad's silence was eloquent. Clark shook his head, just a little. His dad had a good sense of people. If he felt Jed Franklin could snap, then maybe he could.

Clark's dad grabbed the coffee pot, poured himself a cup, and came back to the table.

"Let's just hope I'm wrong," he said.

His neck hurt. His chin rested on his chest, and his lips were so chapped that they stung. His mouth was open and dry. More than thirst. Whatever they had sprayed on him, whatever they had used to knock him out, had left a terrible cottony flavor on his tongue.

Lionel Luthor kept his eyes closed and forced himself to take stock. He'd lost his advantage the last time because his kidnappers realized that he was awake.

He wouldn't make that mistake again.

Obviously, he'd been out for some time. His shoulders still ached, only this time in a different place. He was sitting up on a hard chair. He wasn't dizzy, and he had no sense of movement. Apparently, they had arrived at their destination.

He wondered where it was. By keeping him unconscious, they'd ruined his sense of time. He had no idea if he was close to Metropolis or not, if they'd flown him somewhere, if they'd merely driven him in circles.

He wouldn't be able to help anyone find him—provided he got free.

They didn't have his mouth bound. That was a bad sign. It meant he could yell all he wanted to, and his kidnappers thought no one would hear him.

He couldn't think of any place in Metropolis like that, a place where a person would be absolutely certain no one could hear. Even the best soundproofing let an occasional loud noise out.

If he were a betting man—and he was not; he believed in making fortunes, not squandering them—he would wager he was in the country somewhere, somewhere with a lot of wide-open space around him, no neighbors and no busy roads.

Kansas had a lot of places like that. Come to think of it, so did much of America.

He was back where he started. He could be anywhere.

He suppressed a sigh and went back to his inventory. His hands were tied behind him, the bonds so tight that they cut into his skin. His feet were separated, his knees open, and his ankles were tied to something—probably the legs of the chair he was sitting on.

The room smelled of dust and mold, and carried the remaining heat of the wretched April afternoon. Luthor caught no food odors, no pet scents, no garbage smells.

The place had been abandoned, or was little used. Maybe a garage or a storage building, a hunting cabin, something far away from the road.

Somewhere nearby a man was snoring. Deep rumbling snores, punctuated by grunts and an occasional snort. The sound of someone in a sound sleep. Luthor didn't hear footsteps or a television. He couldn't hear ambient road noise or any other sound from outside.

Just the snoring.

Could his captors be that careless? Could they have brought him here—wherever here was—and left him with a sleeping guard?

Or were they testing him, trying to see if he was as ingenious as everyone said he was?

Ultimately, it didn't matter. In the end, these guys would kill him. That's what kidnappers did. Even if they weren't planning to initially, they would come to the realization that Luthor knew too much about them, that he no longer had any value to them.

If the ransom was paid, they'd return his corpse.

If it wasn't—and those were the instructions he always gave his subordinates, not to waste wealth on sentimentality—then his kidnappers would get impatient and kill him.

Escape. Survival. They were both up to him.

He opened his eyes enough to peer through his eyelashes. A small light burned on a teetering end table. On a ratty couch, a man sprawled, his arm over his eyes. The snorer, wearing ragged blue jeans and a flannel shirt that was too heavy for the day's weather. His boots, covered in mud, rested on the couch's arm.

Luthor couldn't tell if he'd seen the man before or not. The man was a type—thin face, a few days' growth of beard, scraggly hair in need of a cut. All the man needed was a pickup truck and a mangy dog, and he'd fit Luthor's definition of "redneck" perfectly.

The only thing missing was the empty beer cans on the scuffed wooden floor.

Luthor held his breath, wishing the snoring would stop. He couldn't hear anyone else breathe or even move, but he didn't trust his ears. The snorer was a symphony of noise—sound after sound, often without a pause.

Still, Luthor hadn't seen anyone else. The light from the single lamp was dim. He could risk opening his eyes all the way, if he didn't move his head.

He eased his eyes open, and found himself staring at the scuffed wooden floor. Mud caked it. Not all of the mud went to the shoes of the snorer. Some of it trailed around Luthor. More of it was gathered around the door, as if people had tracked it in and out.

The mud was still black, too. Not dried yet. He didn't like the looks of that. It meant he was as far out in the country as he thought. A lot of roads off the main highway were either dirt or gravel, and most driveways definitely were. People who lived this poorly usually didn't put concrete sidewalks in either.

He definitely wasn't in Metropolis anymore.

The cabin was small, with a low ceiling and cracked windows caked with filth. The door was improperly hung. He could see light through the frame—a thin electric light, probably some kind of porch light.

So, the snorer was waiting for someone.

Or the cabin was so deep in the country that a single outdoor light wouldn't attract any attention.

Luthor raised his head slowly. The back of his neck cramped and he winced, biting his lower lip so that he didn't cry out in pain. The snorer snorted, sighed, and rolled over, his face colliding with the back of the couch.

He didn't seem to notice.

Luthor looked around. One main room, poorly furnished. A handmade table and chairs stood near the open kitchen. To call the area a kitchen, though, was to give it more dignity than it had. There was a sink, a refrigerator older than Luthor himself, and a small stove, with a coffeepot on top.

It had been decades since Luthor had seen a coffeepot on a stove top. He almost felt as if he had gone back in time.

A thin pink throw rug covered the area in front of the sink. And filthy, threadbare towels hung from a rack hanging on the wall beside the refrigerator.

The sink was spotless, though, and so was the stove. No dishes sat out, and no crumbs covered the meager counter. Either no one had used this place in a long time or someone was neat.

Which didn't explain the mud.

Luthor glanced over his shoulder. An open door led to a small bathroom. Another door opened into what appeared to be a bedroom. He thought he saw the edge of a bed in there, but he couldn't be certain.

An open closet, with a curtain hanging over a bar in place of a door, stood across from the kitchen. There were no other doors in the room. Only the cracked windows and the main entrance.

To get out, Luthor would either have to walk past the snorer or break a window.

Provided, of course, that he could get himself untied.

He wiggled his swollen fingers, feeling the pins and needles creep up his hands. Even though he could touch whatever bound him, he couldn't tell what it was. He didn't have enough feeling in his fingertips.

He looked down at his feet. They were bound with a thick rope. He assumed that his hands were bound the same way.

The thick rope was to his advantage. It wouldn't tie as tightly as a small rope, and he might be able to wriggle free.

The snorer gulped, snorted, then rolled over again. Obviously, his dreams weren't pleasant. Luthor watched, waiting for the man to wake up. When the man didn't, Luthor pulled his hands as far apart as they would go.

The rope dug deeper into his skin, but he thought he felt

a bit of give. Just enough, maybe, that if he worked it, he might be able to free himself.

He had no idea how much time that would take.

He had no idea how much time he had.

But he knew he had to act quickly and decisively. It was the only way to get free.

CHAPTER SEVEN

The door to the *Torch* office stood open, and the lights burned at every desk even though full morning light poured in the windows. The sunlight hit the Wall of Weird, turning photographs of the meteor rocks a luminescent green.

Clark walked in. He was worried. He hadn't seen Chloe all morning.

She had even missed first period English, the class she loved the most.

"Chloe?" he called.

Her book bag rested against a desk. Her purse hung from the side of an empty chair. Her camera was hooked up to one of the computers, which had a sign on its screen that blinked, *download completed, download completed.*

Clark's stomach clenched. It wasn't like Chloe to be so silent. After losing Danny and Betty Franklin yesterday, Clark was beginning to believe that anyone could disappear.

"Chloe?"

"She's down in the girls' locker room." Lana's soft voice behind Clark made him jump.

He turned. Lana was leaning against the door, hugging her books to her chest. She wore a loose long-sleeved shirt, hip-hugger blue jeans, and sandals, in deference to yesterday's weather. It wasn't supposed to be as warm today, but it hadn't been supposed to get that hot yesterday either.

"The locker room? What's she doing there?"

"Cleaning up." Lana stepped inside the *Torch* office and leaned on one of the computer desks. "She spent the night here."

"Doing what?" Clark asked.

"Looking up stuff on the Franklin case. She was checking disappearances off that property in the past, looking for ghosts, you know the basic stuff." Lana's eyes twinkled, but there were deep circles under them. Even though she seemed better than she had been the day before, she was clearly still bothered by Danny Franklin's death.

"Did she find anything?"

Lana shrugged. "I have no idea. I found her here this morning. She'd fallen asleep. So I loaned her a fresh shirt from my locker, and she went down to take a shower."

"She left her purse," Clark said. Seeing the purse had made him panic. Girls never left their purses behind.

"I know. I was coming up here for it." Lana walked around Clark and picked up the purse. "I was supposed to lock up the *Torch* office, too."

"Probably a good idea," he said.

"What is?" Pete Ross peered around the door, his familiar face squinched in a frown.

"Locking up," Lana said.

"Where's Chloe?" Pete asked, coming inside.

"Long story," Clark said.

"I got some of it from the local news. The day I decide to stick around school to finish my lab project is the day you guys stumble on some excitement."

"It wasn't excitement, Pete." Lana's voice got even softer than normal. "It was horrible."

Pete bit his lower lip. "I'm sorry, Lana. I didn't mean it that way. I just meant—"

"We know what you meant." Clark smoothed over the moment as best he could. Pete hadn't known Danny Franklin as well as Lana had. Clark had a hunch that Pete and Danny had had a run-in a few years ago. They never spoke. "Why're you looking for Chloe?"

"Actually," Pete said, "I was looking for you. Did you hear about Lex?"

"What about him?" Lana asked before Clark could.

"His dad's been kidnapped." Pete didn't sound too distressed about it. But Pete wasn't too fond of the Luthors. "Lex flew out of here yesterday afternoon."

"To Metropolis?" Clark asked.

"Yeah. His dad was taken from there. In front of a bank, of all things. They took his limo. You really hadn't heard?"

Clark shook his head. He hadn't paid attention to the news, and he'd been thinking about the Franklin murders. He wondered how Lex was doing. Lex and his father didn't get along, but it was obvious Lex cared about his dad. This had to be really difficult.

"I would've thought you were going with him," Pete said to Clark.

"Why would I have gone with him?"

"Because you two are friends." Pete made the statement sound casual, but they both knew it wasn't. Pete had been feeling left out of Clark's life lately, mostly because of Lex.

"I was a little busy yesterday," Clark said. "I hadn't heard about Lex's dad at all."

"What happened?" Lana asked.

"No one knows, exactly," Pete said. He obviously paid attention to the whole story. Pete had never liked the Luthors. He felt that they had betrayed his family when they bought the creamed corn factory from Pete's dad years ago and turned it into a fertilizer plant. "No one's talking either. I don't even know if they got a ransom note."

Clark swallowed, not sure if he wanted to ask the question that popped into his mind. But he had to know. "Are they sure it's a kidnapping?"

"And not a murder?" Pete said. "They're saying kidnapping. But it sounds suspicious to me."

"Poor Lex." Lana hugged her books even tighter. "What must he be going through?"

"Hell, I'd bet."

The three of them started. Chloe was in the doorway. Clark hadn't heard her approach either. Proof that he had a lot to think about. He usually noticed everything around him.

Chloe had stepped just inside the room and pushed the door closed behind her. Her hair was still damp, giving it some extra curl. The shirt she wore seemed too frilly for her. Even if Lana hadn't told Clark that she had given Chloe the shirt, Clark would have known that the shirt didn't belong to Chloe. It didn't suit her at all.

But it did give him a sense of a kinder, gentler Chloe, the person she might have been without that fierce drive, incredible intelligence, and willingness to go the distance for any news story.

She picked up her purse and shook it at Lana. "I'm glad I didn't wait for you."

"I'm sorry," Lana said. "Pete was just telling us about Lex."

"I heard," Chloe said. "The whole school is talking about it."

"Not Danny Franklin?" Clark felt a twinge of sadness, as if Danny couldn't get any attention, not even in death.

"Oh, no," Chloe said. "They're talking about him, too. People are wondering if it's all linked, you know. Bad things happening to anyone connected with Smallville. The usual."

It was usual, that was the sad thing. Clark used to deny it, but he couldn't any longer, not with Chloe's Wall of Weird facing him.

"Do you think they're linked?" Pete asked Chloe.

"I'm not ruling anything out." She slung her purse over her shoulder, then paused at the computer that had been downloading the photographs from her camera. She moved the mouse, clicked off the alert, and backed up the pictures on a CD.

"That makes sense." Pete leaned on a nearby desk. "Wasn't it Sherlock Holmes who said there is no such thing as a coincidence?"

"I think the phrase is more modern than that." Lana moved toward Chloe, watching her work. "But I don't remember offhand which detective coined it."

"I thought it was Holmes," Pete said without rancor.

"Trust Lana," Clark said. "She's read everything, it seems."

She gave him a warm smile. "Not everything, Clark. Although that's one of my goals."

"Impossible goal," Chloe said, moving toward her main computer. "They keep publishing new books all the time."

"I'm just trying to get through my parents' collection of old paperbacks. With a side journey for the occasional new book that catches my eye." Lana leaned forward, squinting at Chloe's computer. "What're you doing?"

"Calling up information on the kidnapping. I didn't hear where it happened, did you?"

"Metropolis," Pete said. "Outside City Bank. It was a pretty big deal."

"Metropolis," Chloe muttered. She clicked the mouse a few times. Clark saw screen after screen of information appear on the computer. "Well, that's frustrating."

"What is?" Lana asked. "I don't see anything."

"He was abducted in his own limo." Chloe sat down in the wooden desk chair behind the computer.

"So?" Pete asked. "What were you expecting?"

Clark came forward, setting his books on a nearby desk. "She was hoping that there would have been a one-ton pickup involved, preferably a red one, about ten years old."

Chloe gave him a quick grin over her shoulder. "No moss grows on you."

"Huh?" Pete asked.

"I don't know," Lana said, "but I'm guessing that the pickup belongs to the Franklin family. Chloe was hoping for an obvious connection."

"I'll still settle for this one, though," Chloe said. "I think it's suspicious that the crimes happened on the same day."

"Good thing you're not a cop," Pete said. "You'd try to link a purse-snatching in Los Angeles to a bank robbery in London just because they occurred on the same date."

"If I were a cop," Chloe said, "at least one of those would be out of my jurisdiction."

She continued to type as she spoke, the keys making clicking noises that echoed in the room.

"Has there been any word on the rest of the family?" Clark asked.

Chloe shook her head. "And the police are searching everything. No one has any idea what's going on."

"It's just so sad," Lana said. "I'm trying not to think about it. But I keep wondering who'll take care of Danny. You know, the funeral and everything."

"There's other family," Pete said. "They're just out of state. I'm sure they're on the way here."

"If they're not hiding Mr. and Mrs. Franklin and Bonnie," Chloe said.

"I sure wish we knew what happened," Clark said.

"Well, I know what's going to happen to us if we don't make third period," Pete said. "You skip more than one class with Mr. Gates, and you get detention."

"I've never skipped a class with Mr. Gates," Clark said.

"You're not the one I'm worried about." Pete flashed him a grin. "Let's go."

He headed for the door, but Clark didn't follow immediately. As he grabbed his books off the desk, he said, "You're going to class today, aren't you, Chloe?"

"As soon as I find what I'm looking for," she said.

"You know that Principal Kwan won't let you continue with the *Torch* if your grades go down."

"My grades won't go down, Clark," Chloe said. "I've already read all my textbooks. Sometimes I feel like I could give the lectures myself."

Clark shook his head, but he knew better than to push her. He joined Pete in the hallway. Lana followed.

"Sometimes I wonder why I study so hard," she said, "when things come so easily to Chloe."

"They don't grade life on a curve, Lana," Clark said, leading the three of them down the empty hall. Second period hadn't let out yet, but the *Torch* office was pretty far from the chemistry lab.

"I wish they did," Lana said. "At least then I'd understand the rules."

She peeled off and headed for her locker. Pete stared after her. "What did that mean?"

"I have a hunch she was thinking about Lex's dad and Danny Franklin," Clark said.

"I don't think what happened to Danny had anything to do with rules," Pete said.

Clark nodded, but he found himself thinking about that comment all during Mr. Gates's chemistry lab. Something didn't fit. But Clark wasn't sure yet what that something was.

Lex Luthor stood in the loading zone outside of City Bank. The area wasn't cordoned off—too busy for that kind of nonsense, the obnoxious police detective had told him—

but Lex had gotten some of the security people to keep crowds and traffic away.

He wanted to see the place for himself.

He'd already seen it on the bank security tape. Several video cameras filmed the loading zone, the sidewalk, and the parking areas as a matter of course.

He had spent the night viewing the tapes, reviewing the events, and waiting for the kidnappers to contact him with a ransom. The police and the FBI were there as well, with their phone-tapping equipment and their instructions.

Lex had been ignoring the so-called authorities. They weren't relevant to him. The statistics—with or without police involvement—did not favor his father. Most kidnappers killed their victims within the first forty-eight hours.

Twenty-four of those forty-eight were nearly up, and no one had made any progress.

Lex scanned the area. It looked so different than it had the afternoon before, and not just because the security tapes were in grainy black-and-white. The limo wasn't there, of course, and the crowds seemed thinner. A lot of people were stopping to gawk. Apparently they knew who he was. They probably wondered what he was trying to do.

Too bad no one had watched when his father was kidnapped. The police had canvassed the area, tried to identify faces off the security tape, and had released pleas for assistance from the general public.

As usual, no one saw anything. At least, no one who saw anything was coming forward. If Lex had to, he would find a way around that. Money always talked.

He walked the short distance from the bank doors to the loading zone. So easy. It only took him a few seconds. The crowd watched him, unusually silent. His security people—or rather, his father's security people—watched as well.

They apparently had no idea what he was doing. He wasn't about to enlighten them.

He checked the ground for glass vials, spray canisters, anything that could have caused three grown men to hit the ground in a matter of seconds. The bystanders also got hit, which meant that whatever the kidnappers had used to knock everyone out—and they were knocked out—had been airborne.

No one had been seriously injured, at least from the knockout gas (a few people had been trampled after they fell, and a few others had hit their heads rather hard), but medical personnel couldn't identify the chemical used.

It was making treatment difficult, or so they told Lex, because they were afraid of drug interactions. They found no strange chemicals in the bloodstream of the people who went down. The doctors also took nose and throat swabs, and they were hoping to get something from that.

But those results might take days.

Lex knew his father didn't have days.

Lex rubbed his eyes. He hadn't slept all night. He reviewed the surveillance tapes, went over his father's files, looked through the threatening letters and e-mails that his father constantly received.

Even though he knew his father had enemies, Lex was stunned by the vitriol his father received day in and day out. It was a wonder that his father wasn't more cautious than he was. With that much hatred coming at his father, it was a wonder that his father went outside at all.

But it did explain his father's complete lack of interest in the unrest at the Smallville facility. The stuff that Lex had been calling him about every day was nothing compared with things his father had dealt with in Metropolis alone all month.

Brown glass winked against the curb. Lex crouched and

examined the shards. They were thick—the kind of glass used in beer bottles. After a moment, he saw the neck of the bottle, farther down the curb, resting uncomfortably over a sewer grate.

Nothing. No evidence that anything had happened here.

He was at loose ends and he felt like he was fighting this alone. His father's security people didn't seem to know what they were doing. The police and the FBI were following the official handbook, taking everything one worthless step at a time.

They might find the kidnappers, but they would do so long after Lionel Luthor was dead.

Lex stood and surveyed the small stretch of road where his father had vanished. Large stone buildings that had stood on that site since the end of the nineteenth century faced him, their windows barred off so that no one could break in from outside. Around the corner, a taxi stand, and a little farther beyond that, a bus stop.

He would wager his entire inheritance that no one thought to canvass people on the other side of the street.

He signaled Harrison. The man, with the burly look of an ex–football player going slowly to fat, lumbered over.

"Mr. Luthor?"

Lex pointed at the buildings. "See those windows over there?"

"Yes, sir."

"I want every person with a view out those windows to be interviewed about my father's disappearance. I want the interviews to cover the three days previous to the disappearance all the way through this morning. I want to know everything that happened, however trivial. If some squirrel dropped a nut down that sewer grate, I want to know about it. You got that?"

"Yes, sir." Harrison had been amazingly humble since Lex had arrived, as if he were afraid of being fired.

Lex was withholding judgment on firing his father's people. If they could redeem themselves by finding his father, he would let them keep their jobs.

But he didn't trust that they would. He had his own network here in Metropolis. Younger guys, people he had befriended in boarding school, people whose characters weren't as pristine as his father would like.

Lex also had feelers out with them. If they heard anything, they would let Lex know. They knew he could match or double any amount anyone else would pay for silence.

Lex would find his father, one way or another.

The only worry that Lex had was whether or not he would find his father before it was too late.

CHAPTER EIGHT

Lionel Luthor had worked maybe a quarter of an inch of give into the ropes that bound his hands when the snorer woke up. The man snorted, choked, and sat up, clutching his forehead as if it hurt him.

"Honey?" he said, his voice deep and raw.

Luthor didn't move. He kept his hands as far apart as they would go so that it didn't seem like the ropes were loose.

The man didn't seem to notice him. Not right away. The man blinked, then rubbed his eyes with the heel of his hand.

For a moment, Luthor thought the man might lie back down, but he didn't.

The man had slept later than Luthor thought he would. The sun had been up for some time. Light poured into the windows behind Luthor, revealing the filth and the mouse droppings that mixed with the mud on the scuffed wooden floor.

No one else had arrived at the cabin, and Luthor couldn't see out the windows in front of him. He had no idea if there was a car or any other mode of transportation out there.

He had no idea what he'd do once he got free of his ropes.

After a moment, the man pivoted, put his feet on the floor, and groaned. Then he got up, adjusted his blue jeans, and started toward the bathroom. Halfway there, he saw Luthor.

Their gazes met. The man looked defeated, as if he were the prisoner instead of Luthor.

The man skirted around the chair without saying a word.

Luthor waited until the man reached the bathroom door before saying, “You know, I have to do that, too.”

The man sighed, leaned his head forward, and somehow managed to look even more defeated. “That’s not my problem.”

“It will be,” Luthor said. “I am known for my rigid control, but after a while, even the most rigid control gives way to the inevitable.”

“Whatever.” The man went into the bathroom and closed the door.

Luthor closed his eyes in frustration. If he could get the man to undo at least one of his hands, he might have a chance. He wouldn’t be able to push much, though. He was, after all, the one with the disadvantage.

He would just have to find a way to turn that disadvantage into an opportunity. He’d spent his life doing that. Turning a man like this one—clearly the flunky of the three who kidnapped him—shouldn’t be hard.

If he had the time to finesse it.

Luthor glanced at the windows. Still nothing from outside. And then the water turned on in the bathroom. A shower? The man seemed awfully trusting of Luthor.

Luthor smiled for the first time that day.

Maybe gaining an advantage would be easier than he thought.

Chloe hadn’t shown up for geometry. Clark finished the last problem on the pop quiz, then double-checked his work. Since this geometry class was in the last period of the day, the teacher let the students turn in their quizzes and leave.

Pete had just finished, too. He stood up, took the quiz to

the front of the room, and handed it to the teacher. Clark followed.

Lana wasn't in this class. She had geometry earlier in the day. Her final class of the day was social studies, and that teacher rarely let anyone leave before the bell.

Pete waited for Clark up front. They left the classroom together, sliding into the wide, empty corridor, before saying anything. Even then, they kept their voices down. If they got caught talking too loudly, their open-classroom privileges would be revoked.

"Chloe's going to be really cheesed that she missed a pop quiz," Pete said.

"Maybe she can make it up," Clark said.

"No makeups if you attended other classes that day, remember? We got her to go to chem."

"So she's going to be upset at us," Clark said. "And here I was going to suggest we go to the *Torch* office to see what else she found."

"It better be the news story of the century," Pete said, "because the 4.0 she's been working on this quarter just got shot."

Clark nodded. He wondered if Chloe would even think about that—at least at this point. She'd notice later, when the story was over.

He and Pete moved silently through the hallways. The classroom doors were all closed, and through the small square windows in each, Clark could see teachers moving back and forth near their desks. In some rooms, students sat attentively in the front rows, and in others, chaos seemed to reign.

As he passed the social studies room, he saw Lana hand a note to a friend, who read the note, looked over at Lana, and grinned.

"You're hopeless, you know that?" Pete slapped a hand on Clark's back. "Let's move on."

He was hopeless. He did know that. And sometimes he thought Lana actually noticed how interested he was and returned that interest. Then he'd listen to her talk about Whitney and what he was doing in the Marines, and realize that she still thought of Clark as nothing more than the boy next door.

He and Pete arrived in the *Torch* office a few minutes later. Sure enough, Chloe was at her favorite computer, pounding on the keys.

"Any developments?" Clark asked as he set his books on a nearby desk.

Chloe jumped half a foot and put a hand over her heart. "Jeez, Clark. Hello would be nice."

"I don't think you would have heard me if I was polite," Clark said.

"Yeah," Pete said, pulling a chair beside Chloe. "I suspect someone could have told you any old thing, and unless it was related to the Franklin case, you wouldn't have noticed."

"I'd have noticed if there was anything on the Luthor kidnapping." Chloe started typing again. She was on the Internet. An ad flashed on top of her screen, followed by lots of text.

"So nothing's changed?" Clark asked.

"For the Luthors or the Franklins?" Chloe asked, not taking her gaze off the screen.

"Luthors," Clark said as Pete said, "Franklins."

"No," Chloe said. "Nothing's changed."

"For which?" Pete asked.

"Luthors," Chloe said. "There hasn't even been word of a ransom note."

"That's not good." Pete no longer sounded pleased about the Luthor kidnapping.

"No, it's not," Clark said. He wondered if he could get ahold of Lex. Of course, if he did manage to speak to Lex, he had no idea what he'd say. From this distance, there was really nothing he could do.

Besides, this was one of those cases where Clark agreed with his father: The authorities were better off handling the kidnapping. At least until they had a suspect. Then maybe Clark could find a way to help that wouldn't be noticed.

The past twenty-four hours had been very frustrating to him. He hadn't been able to help Danny or Betty Franklin, and right now, there wasn't anything he could do for Lex either. Yet he felt like he should be able to do something.

Clark grabbed a chair and pulled it up to Chloe's other side. "What are you doing?"

She leaned forward so that she blocked his view of the screen. "Working."

"I figured that much out. On what?"

She was too thin to hide the screen from both Clark and Pete, and she knew it. She looked first at Clark, then at Pete, and sighed. "Go close the door, one of you, okay?"

Pete was closest. He got up and pushed the door closed. "Okay," he said as he walked back to his chair. "Spill."

"I've been monitoring the news reports." Chloe lifted a small Walkman from inside her purse. The movement made a tiny cord that she had hidden under her blouse move so that Clark could see it. The cord led to her left ear. "They've got a theory about the crime."

"The Franklin thing," Pete said, "not the Luthor thing, right?"

"Right," Chloe said. She put the Walkman back and

grabbed the mouse. She hit "sleep" so that the screen she had up completely disappeared.

"And?" Clark said. "What's the theory?"

"They think Jed Franklin killed his whole family."

Clark started. His father had said the same thing last night.

Pete made a face. "Why would a guy do that?"

"I don't know the whys," Chloe said. "Just that they have some reports of him acting suspicious before the bodies were found. And someone claims to have seen him after the official time of death for Danny."

"Someone?" Clark said.

Chloe gave him a sheepish look. "I was in French."

"In other words, you missed it," Pete said.

"I missed it," Chloe said. "I figure it'll repeat."

"Meanwhile, you were looking for the same story on the Internet," Clark said.

"Not exactly." Chloe crossed her arms. "Look, if I tell you guys what I was doing, we could all get in trouble."

"I don't care about getting in trouble," Pete said. "Do you, Clark?"

Actually, Clark did. Whenever Chloe had such concerns, she had done something very wrong. Sometimes against-the-law kind of wrong.

"What did you do?" he asked Chloe, dodging Pete's question.

"Have you ever met Jed Franklin?" Chloe asked, dodging Clark's question.

Apparently, no one was going to give straight answers this afternoon.

"Not that I remember," Clark said. "Lana said he seemed nice. My mom called him gentle."

But Clark's father thought he'd seen darkness in Mr. Franklin. Only Clark didn't tell Chloe that.

"That's how I always felt about him, too. If anything, I got the sense that he wasn't strong enough to stand up to people. And that included Mrs. Franklin."

"Guys like that snap," Pete said. "You got to watch out for the quiet ones. You know, like our buddy Clark here."

Clark felt his cheeks warm. "I'm not quiet."

"You're not loud either," Pete said. "Sometimes getting a read on you is difficult."

"But that's my point," Chloe said. "Clark's gentle, too. And he wouldn't do anything like this."

"You hope," Pete said.

"I'm being serious, Pete." Chloe frowned at him.

Pete studied her for a minute, then nodded. "Sorry. I'm not handling all this stuff too well. It's easier to joke about it."

"A lot has happened the last few days," Clark said.

"I don't like any of it," Pete said.

"And that's my point." Chloe grabbed the notebook she kept beside the computer. She opened it to a page covered with her handwriting.

Clark stared at it. Chloe hated taking notes by hand, considering it very old-fashioned. She did it when she had to, but she tried to avoid it at all costs.

"Their theory of the crime," Chloe said, still paging through her notebook, "is that he did it. Mine was that the family was on the run."

"Was?" Pete asked.

Chloe held up a finger to silence him. "According to my source in the sheriff's office—"

"You have a source?" Pete asked.

"A deputy who thinks she's cute," Clark said. "Hasn't she told you that?"

"That she's cute?" Pete asked.

"That she flirted her way out of a ticket and has been using the poor guy ever since."

Chloe elbowed Clark in the side. "Stop it. I'm trying to be serious here."

"Just catching Pete up on the facts."

Pete grinned at Clark. "Facts a man can use."

Clark nodded.

"Guys," Chloe said. "This is important."

"Sorry," Pete said, and leaned forward. "Go on, Ms. Woodward."

"I think in this mood, she's Bernstein," Clark said.

"*According to my source,*" Chloe said, talking over them, "the police have some information that we don't have."

"That's a surprise," Pete said.

"*Like,*" Chloe said with even more force, "the fact that Mr. Franklin was seen in Smallville as recently as two days ago."

"By the mysterious someone," Pete said, clearly becoming serious again.

"You said that was on the radio," Clark said.

"Part of it was," Chloe said. "But not the part about Smallville, and not the fact that it was a reliable witness—and no, I wasn't able to get the name. My source also says that Mr. Franklin was arrested three times in the last month for being drunk and disorderly. He actually tore up a bar."

"I thought you said he was gentle." Pete was frowning.

"I pushed on this point, and it turns out that 'tore up' means he knocked over some glasses and a table when he passed out. Of course, he'd been shouting before that about how much he hated LuthorCorp, and that really upset a lot of people, but there's no more than that." Chloe still hadn't looked in her notebook, although she'd stopped thumbing through the pages.

"They're basing the idea that he killed his family on that?" Clark asked.

"And a couple of other things," Chloe said. "Apparently Danny and Betty didn't drown. They were both strangled, and Danny had a lot of bruises on his hands and arms, as if he'd been pummeling someone, trying to get free. Neither of them was bound or gagged, and they weren't suffocated with a pillow or anything. Whoever killed them used his hands."

"You'd have to be pretty strong to do that," Pete said.

"Not to mention determined." Clark shook his head. He was strong, and he couldn't imagine killing anyone in that way. "This doesn't make any sense. To do that, you'd have to be looking your victim in the face."

"One point for the psycho-killer theory," Pete said.

"I've been doing some research on the Internet," Chloe said, "and there's been a lot written on this topic, especially lately because there's been so many instances of a parent murdering the entire family. Besides that woman in Texas, there've been cases in Georgia, Oregon—"

"We do follow the news, Chloe," Clark said gently.

She nodded, but barely took a breath before continuing. "Anyway, what all of these killers have in common was that they thought they were sending their families to a better place. It was, for them, an act of love."

"Yeah, right." Pete stood up. "That's a bunch of —"

The door opened, and Pete stopped. Lana looked in. "I thought I'd find you guys here. Is there more news?"

"We're trying to find that out from Chloe," Clark said. "It's turning out to be surprisingly difficult."

Lana grinned.

"Come in or stay out," Chloe said, "but either way, close the door."

Pete whistled. "You are uptight, girl."

"I've got more to tell you," Chloe said, "and I really don't want the entire school to know."

"Sounds serious." Lana came inside, closing the door tightly behind her. She pulled a chair over and joined the group. "So what have I missed? I need all the gossip."

Chloe's mouth was a thin line, and she was tapping her right foot.

Lana looked at her, then glanced at Clark, eyes twinkling.

"Yeah, Clark and I tried the gossip thing already," Pete said. "Chloe's having none of it, even if it was her cop boyfriend we were talking about."

"You have a boyfriend who is a policeman?" Lana asked. She sounded impressed.

Chloe shot Pete a dark look. Clark wondered why she hadn't aimed it at him. After all, he was the one who spilled the secret.

"He's a source, that's all."

"Is it that deputy?" Lana asked. "I've seen him around. He's cute."

Chloe's eyes narrowed. Clark recognized the expression. She was going to blow soon.

"Where were we?" Clark asked, to avoid more fireworks.

"Some idiotic theory about people murdering their families out of love," Pete said.

"Ick." Lana frowned. "They think Mr. Franklin did it? I don't believe that. He's so nice."

"I don't even remember why you were making that point, Chloe," Pete said.

"Because," Clark said, "I mentioned that to kill someone that way, you'd have to look them in the face. I didn't think a father could do that. But if he did it out of love—"

"No." Lana shook her head. "Mr. Franklin isn't crazy. There aren't a lot of people who love their families as much as he did. He would never do something like this."

"Someone did, Lana," Pete said.

"I don't think it was Mr. Franklin either," Chloe said.

"Yeah." Clark glanced at her notebook again. "You said you had a different theory of the crime."

"I think 'had' is the operative word," Pete said. "She was using past tense."

Chloe nodded, then graced Pete with a smile. The smile relieved Clark. It meant that Chloe was calming down.

"I did have a different theory, and I found some stuff that disproved my theory and the police's." She glanced over her shoulder at the door. "That's why I didn't want us overheard."

"Because of your theory?" Pete asked.

"No," Chloe said. "Because of the work I did to disprove it."

"You'd better catch me up," Lana said. "I'm not sure what your theory was."

"I hadn't told them yet, either," Chloe said.

Lana looked at Clark. He nodded his agreement.

Chloe stood up and checked the windows, talking as she moved around the room. "I developed part of the theory while we were at the Franklin farm. Remember, I said that it seemed odd to me that the car was gone. I was hoping the other three members of the family escaped."

"You're using past tense again, Chloe," Pete said.

Chloe nodded. She checked the closet door, then stopped in front of the Wall of Weird. She put a hand on it as if it gave her strength.

"After I talked to my source—"

"The cute deputy," Clark said.

"—I decided to do some digging." Chloe glared at Clark.

He got the message. He would remain quiet. But he felt like Pete had; he couldn't take the seriousness. He needed to lighten the mood just a little. Otherwise, the facts of the last day might overwhelm him.

"I figured if the family was on the move, I'd be able to track them," Chloe said.

"How?" Lana asked.

"They'd have to get money somewhere. I figured there'd at least be a big withdrawal from their checking account. Maybe they'd even use checks or their credit cards. But nothing turned up," Chloe said.

"Chloe." Clark spoke before he could stop himself. "That's illegal."

She raised her eyebrows at him.

"Hence the closed door," Lana said.

"How'd you know how to do that?" Pete asked.

"I wish I could say it was hard," Chloe said.

"Don't you think the police would do the same thing?" Clark asked.

"After they got warrants and orders and legal stuff, sure," Chloe said. "I suspect I'm ahead of them."

"And you didn't find anything?" Pete asked.

"Nothing." Chloe sat down. She picked up her notebook. "Their accounts are a mess though. They have less than two hundred dollars combined in their checking and savings account. Their credit cards are maxed, and the bank canceled their line of credit."

"That had to create a lot of pressure," Lana said.

Chloe nodded.

"If everything's maxed," Clark said, "then they wouldn't be able to use their credit cards."

"I did find a gas card that Mr. Franklin had been using for the farm equipment and his truck. That card wasn't maxed, and it would have gotten them quite a ways out of Smallville. It hasn't been touched at all."

"They could have been using cash," Pete said.

"From where?" Chloe asked. "They haven't made a withdrawal."

"A lot of farm families in the Midwest got into the habit of keeping their money in a safe at home. My grandfather says it went back to the Depression," Pete said.

"That was a long time ago," Clark said. "We're a farm family. We use the bank like normal people."

"I don't think they had money in a safe at home or under the mattress or whatever fantasy you want to concoct," Lana said. "It was really clear to me that Danny was panicked when we were assigned the lab experiment. We had to buy lab equipment, and Danny couldn't afford lunch every day. Remember, Clark? That day he was kicking the candy machine?"

Clark nodded. The candy machine in the lunchroom had eaten a dollar and not given Danny the candy bar he'd wanted. He kicked the machine so hard it dented.

Lana had talked to Danny, while Clark surreptitiously repaired the dent with his super strength. He didn't want Danny to get into more trouble than he would already be in.

That day, Lana had shared her lunch with Danny. Clark wondered how many other times she had done that.

"He was pretty upset about losing a dollar. I can't imagine him being that way if the family had a stash," Lana said.

"Provided he knew about it," Pete said.

"I think he knew everything there was to know about the family money," Chloe said. "He was the one managing most of the farm stuff while his dad worked at LuthorCorp. That was pretty clear from the financial records, too."

"Maybe they pawned stuff," Pete said. "The Franklins have lived in that house for generations. When you live someplace that long, old junk turns into collectibles after a while."

Chloe shook her head. "If they had stuff to pawn, they would have done it a long time ago. When the bank cut off their credit, or something."

"That makes sense," Clark said. "They had to pay for seed and fertilizer and gas just to keep the farm running. Usually the bank fronts that stuff and the farmer pays it back later. If they didn't have a credit line, they had to get the money from somewhere. Those fields had been tilled. You don't do that if you have nothing to plant."

"Okay," Lana said, leaning back. "I'm confused then. Where does that leave us?"

"With two incorrect theories of the crime," Chloe said. "I don't think Mr. Franklin did it—after all, he'd need money, too."

"But Chloe, it's easier for one person to run than three," Pete said. "Maybe he's been stealing to survive."

Chloe shook her head. "The police have his car description and license plate number. They've gotten no hits on it so far, and they've publicized that part to pieces. They've had a few false positives on the truck, but when they checked it out, it was pretty clear that they didn't have the right one."

"The family couldn't have split up?" Pete asked.

This time, Clark shook his head. "Not if something this traumatic happened. Think about it, Pete."

"I have been." Pete crossed his arms. "I have been ever since I heard about it. I don't like any of it."

"Me, either," Lana said.

Chloe looked at the Wall of Weird. "Just when you think you've seen everything—"

"But this isn't something for the Wall of Weird, is it?" Pete asked. "I mean this happens other places, not just Smallville."

"The first true crime novel ever written was about the

murder of a family in Kansas," Lana said. "It's called *In Cold Blood*."

"What happened?" Clark asked.

Lana's gaze met his for just a moment. "That's the sad thing. It was so senseless. These two thieves heard there was a lot of money in this farmhouse, so they broke in, and killed the entire family, but didn't find any of the money they were searching for."

"Do you think that's what happened here?" Pete asked.

"It's a possibility," Chloe said.

Clark frowned. He stood up and walked to the Wall of Weird. Mutated frogs, meteorites, green rocks. He could deal with all that. He was having a lot of trouble with senseless violence.

"If that's what happened," he said, "then why hide the bodies in the pond? Why not just leave them where you killed them?"

"And why strangle them instead of shoot them?" Pete asked.

"That's the key," Chloe said.

"Strangling them?" Lana asked.

Chloe shook her head. "Hiding the bodies. That's why the police think it was Mr. Franklin. They thought he wanted to hide his crime."

"Makes sense to me," Pete said.

"But hiding the bodies is the act of a rational person, not an irrational one," Chloe said. "Most of these family murderers kill everyone—"

"With a gun," Lana said.

Clark looked at her in surprise.

She shrugged. "I read a lot. And for a while, I read a lot of true crime. It felt like an escape from all the strange stuff in Smallville."

"Some escape," Pete said.

"But Lana's right," Chloe said. "Usually these guys—and for the most part it is guys—shoot their entire family, and then shoot themselves. But there's no evidence of a shotgun blast in that house."

"And there's no way Mr. Franklin committed those murders if he was rational," Lana said. "I don't care how much evidence someone gathers. I'll never believe that."

"So," Pete said. "What kind of rational person would murder two teenagers and hide them in a pond?"

Clark frowned. "Someone who felt he had something to gain from it."

"What do you gain from murdering high school students?" Lana asked.

"Leverage," Chloe said.

Pete nodded. "If you want a man to do something, threaten his family."

"But who would do that to Mr. Franklin?" Lana asked.

"It goes back to the money," Chloe said. "It always goes back to the money."

"You think he borrowed from someone he shouldn't have?" Pete asked.

"I can't believe there's a mobster-style loan shark in Smallville," Lana said.

"Maybe not Smallville," Clark said, thinking of all the shady things Lex had told him about. "But I'll bet there's a lot of them in Metropolis."

Chloe walked back to her desk and picked up her notebook. "If someone was doing that to Mr. Franklin, he'd leave a trail. He'd be all over Smallville searching for money, for help any way he could get it."

The group was silent. Clark glanced again at the Wall of Weird. Something didn't fit. There was some piece that none of them had looked at, some aspect that they knew about but weren't seeing.

"Then we're back to square one," Pete said.

On the side of the Wall of Weird, Chloe had tacked a map of Smallville and the surrounding areas. She had pushpins stuck all over it in various colors: a large green one where the meteor went down; smaller green ones where meteor rocks had been found; different colors for some of the stranger news stories that had come out of Smallville.

She hadn't marked the Franklin farm yet.

"What are you looking at, Clark?" Lana asked.

He didn't answer her. Instead, he took a step closer to the map. "Is this a current map, Chloe?"

"Last year's," she said. "Why?"

"Did the police search the entire farm?"

"Of course," Chloe said.

"Including the second pond?"

"What second pond?" Chloe asked.

Clark pointed to the map. Hidden in what was now a forest of trees was a small pond. It wouldn't have been visible to someone who didn't know the terrain. It was clear, though, that the second pond had been the main pond back when the farm was smaller.

Chloe came over beside him and studied the map. "I didn't even realize that section was part of the farm."

"Me either until I looked at it," Clark said.

Lana joined them. "It's fenced off. I remember seeing that. Why would that section be fenced off?"

"Farmers fence things a lot, either to keep animals out or to keep them in," Clark said. "I can't tell you how many fences I've helped my dad build trying to keep the deer from my mother's vegetable garden."

"I'll bet the police haven't looked there," Chloe said.

"So maybe we should call them," Pete said.

Chloe shook her head. "Let's check it out ourselves first. We don't want to bother them."

"Not even the cute cop in traffic?" Clark said, only half-teasing.

"Not even him." Chloe was already across the room, gathering her purse and two different cameras. "Come on, you guys. Let's go."

CHAPTER NINE

Even now, Lex could not bring himself to use his father's office as command central. Lex wasn't ready. Maybe someday, if—*when*—he took over LuthorCorp, he would take over this office.

Not until then.

And not in circumstances like these.

Lex passed the door to his father's inner sanctum and went to the large office he'd been using since he arrived in Metropolis. The office was supposed to go to his father's second-in-command. But in all the years that Lex had been paying attention to LuthorCorp, his father never had a second-in-command.

Once upon a time, Lex had thought the office was waiting for him to grow old enough, and experienced enough, to use it. And, if he hadn't known his father better, he might have thought the offer his father had made a few weeks ago—the offer to bring him back to Metropolis—was for the position of second-in-command.

Of course, it hadn't been. It had been because his father was seeing a new side to Lex, a side that had always been there: the dark ruthless side, the side his father had trained into him with all of those years of mind games instead of love.

Lex went inside the office. The room was large, with a standard company desk and a leather-backed rolling desk chair. Empty file cabinets stood against the wall, and a phone with multiple lines sat on the blotter.

The view was spectacular, of course. His father had the best building in one of the highest-rent cities in the world, and the best building had the best view. All of Metropolis spread out before him. Lex could almost imagine himself the Emperor's son, surveying the Empire he would once inherit, should his father die.

Lex clenched a fist. He had been uncertain yesterday, but when he arrived here, he knew his heart. He didn't want his father to die. Not like this. Not kidnapped, powerless, humiliated.

Lex wanted his father to live. Lex wanted to prove to the old man that he could be bested—by his own son. Lex wanted to show Lionel Luthor that underestimating his child was the biggest mistake of his life.

If revenge was a dish best served cold, it was also one made with exquisite care. These kidnappers had interrupted Lex's revenge, petty as it might be.

And if these people turned out to be murderers instead of kidnappers, then they would foil Lex's attempt to worm his way into his father's affections, by proving to his father that he was worthy of his father's love.

Lex allowed himself a small, bitter smile. Self-awareness wasn't all it was cracked up to be. He knew why he was taking these actions; he understood all of his own motivations; and still he despised them. The basis for them all was a childish desire for attention and an even older wish for love.

Sometimes he thought that if he had been raised with parents like Clark Kent's, he wouldn't be this twisted, brilliant man who still hadn't figured out his place in the world. He would know what his place was, and he would feel confident in it.

For even though Lex played at confidence, he lacked it deep down. And even though Clark seemed uncertain at times, he had twenty times the confidence Lex could ever have.

Lex went to the window and looked out. The buildings spread before him like worlds to be conquered. His father was out there somewhere, alive with any kind of luck. All Lex had to do was find him.

With so much money at his fingertips, it was a shock to Lex that he couldn't use it to gain more information. Even his underground connections had nothing.

Well, they had something. They agreed to a person that whoever concocted the scheme to kidnap Lionel Luthor had balls and also that that person was not involved in the Metropolis underworld. No one there wanted to call that kind of attention to himself and his operation.

The theory was that the kidnappers had come in from outside. And, as person after person pointed out to Lex, they had come in prepared.

He walked back to the desk. Even though this office wasn't his, it bore his stamp after twenty-four hours of work. Several empty cappuccino cups, a half-eaten Danish, the remains of a pizza ordered in the middle of the night. Crumpled papers lined the wastebasket, and the blotter was covered with his doodles.

Not to mention the laptop he had placed at the edge of the desk. The computer was one he brought from home. He had several recent models, all of them with programs he needed to scour the Internet for information not on the surface.

Some of his connections in Metropolis were doing the same thing, looking for anything that might link to the kidnapping—a leak of moneys, a passing remark in a chat room, a seemingly innocent query about Lionel Luthor's personal habits. So far, Lex hadn't gotten any reports, but the program he'd set up to do the same thing hadn't come up with anything either.

The silence frustrated him the most and, if he had to be

honest with himself, also worried him the most. Kidnappers with an agenda revealed that agenda. Kidnappers who had no real desire to release their victim often didn't send out ransom notes either.

He sat down at the desk and, with the flick of a thumb, knocked the computer out of sleep mode. An envelope blinked on the side of the screen.

He had missed the alarm notifying him that he had e-mail. He reached for his pager and double-checked it. Nothing there, even though he had set it up for the notification.

His scalp prickled. He supposed if he actually had hair on the back of his neck, it would have risen.

With one shaking finger, he double-clicked the mouse, automatically opening his e-mail program. He had fifty new messages, most of them garbage—reporters, weirdos responding to the news reports, a few internal memos.

But one did catch his eye.

It was from LL, and the message header was also LL. The message had a red exclamation point next to it, marking it as urgent.

Lex realized he was holding his breath. He let the air out slowly, remembering the yoga calming techniques he'd learned at one boarding school or another.

The e-mail had an attachment, and it had gotten through his firewall. Still, he didn't trust that it was virus-free.

He silently cursed himself. He should have brought the e-mail in on a completely clean computer, not one he was running other work on. He could forward it, he supposed, but he decided to take the risk. He would open it.

But first, he ran his antivirus program. It didn't delete the e-mail, so he clicked the e-mail open. It read:

```
Lex Luthor:
  For $30 million you can have your father
back.
  Payouts like this:
  Ten million cash up front.
  Twenty million moved to a numbered
account which we will give you later.
  When the money is safely in our hands,
we will deliver your father to a spot of
our choosing.
  Do not answer this e-mail. We will
contact you.

  P.S. The attachment is proof of our good
intentions.
```

Before clicking on the attachment, Lex disconnected the computer from the office network and unhooked the modem. If the attachment did have a virus or a worm, he wasn't going to send it cascading through the entire corporation.

Once he finished that, he opened the attachments. The first contained several jpeg files, all of them photographs of his father.

The first few came from the limousine, as his father was pushed inside. The next was of his father sitting against a white curtain, his legs sprawled before him, his eyes open but blank.

Lionel Luthor's eyes were never blank.

Lex made himself swallow hard. He needed to get these photographs to someone who could tell him if his father was dead or if he was just doped up. He needed to resolve this—

Then he opened the last attachment. It was a small piece of video. His father, tied to a chair in a darkened room, the camera tight on his face and chest. This morning's *Daily Planet*—the edition that came out just after midnight—

was pinned to his shirt. His father's eyes were closed, his head bobbing up and down like that of a man trying to sleep on an airplane. His chest rose and fell as well.

At that point, at least, his father had been breathing.

Then the video ended. Lex played it again, trying to see anything that might give him a clue as to where his father might be. He didn't recognize anything, but that didn't mean that someone with the proper equipment couldn't find details that would help in the investigation.

He would take this to the computer labs here at Luthor-Corp, as well as to some of his shadier friends. They'd find parts of it that he wouldn't be able to see—a clue, a hint, something.

In all of that material, there had to be something.

Lex saved the e-mail to disk, then closed the laptop. From now on, he would consider it contaminated. He would have to use the backup he had at his apartment to continue the web search.

He slipped the disk into his pocket and stood.

"Mr. Luthor?" His father's secretary stood in the doorway. She was a timid thing, younger than Lex liked, certainly not the standard executive secretary material.

Of course his father had someone else—an older, wiser employee—do the actual office management. Lex had the uncomfortable and unspoken opinion that his father hired pretty secretaries as eye candy or something more.

He didn't want to think about the something more.

"What?" he said in a tone that let her know he was very busy and didn't appreciate the interruption.

"We just got this fax in, sir. I thought you'd want to see it." She extended her hand. In it was a plain sheet of paper. The paper shook.

He grabbed the laptop, slipped it under his arm, and walked over to her. She leaned against the doorframe like a soldier afraid to leave her post. He snatched the fax out of her hand.

The print was slightly blurry—the fax machine needed fresh toner—but the words were easy enough to read.

`Lex Luthor, Check your e-mail`

He looked at the sheet, searching for the originating fax's I.D., but there was nothing obvious.

"Thanks," he said to the secretary.

She raised large brown eyes to his. He saw both fear and worry in them, and he thought it amazing that someone could have those feelings—real feelings—for his father.

"Aren't you going to look at your e-mail?" she asked, her voice shaking.

"I already have." He gave her his warmest smile. "But thanks."

Then he slipped past her, taking the fax with him. Halfway down the hall, he stopped.

"Which fax machine did this come off of?" he asked.

"The one in Mr. Luthor's office."

Of course. Lex nodded. "Make sure no one goes near that machine until I do."

"Yes, sir." She had moved away from the door. "What about the FBI, sir?"

"I'll take care of them," Lex said.

After he took care of other things himself.

Clark sat in the front seat of Chloe's car and stared out the window at the passing trees. Pete and Lana sat in the back, not speaking. Chloe drove carefully for once, perhaps remembering Clark's comments from the day before about cars going into the water.

Amazing how much difference a day made. The weather still hadn't returned to normal, but the intense heat of yesterday afternoon had dissipated. So had Chloe's caution. Instead of parking outside the gate, as she had done the day before, she bounced the car through the ruts left by the police cars and emergency vehicles.

Weeds and rocks scraped the car's undercarriage, but Chloe didn't seem to care. She drove like a woman possessed, convinced that she'd get a scoop yet again.

The pictures in that afternoon's *Torch* had been impressive. To Clark's dismay, the main photo on the front page had been of him pulling Danny's body from the water. The only good part about it had been that the sunlight was behind Clark, putting a halo around the back of his head and placing his face in shadow. Still, anyone who knew him would recognize him.

He hated the notoriety. No matter how much he told Chloe that, she didn't seem to understand it. The story was the story was the story to her. She never thought about the consequences of what she printed.

The consequences in this case would be more than Clark's notoriety as a local boy who did an occasional good deed. The consequences also had to do with his parents, who liked the publicity less than he did.

They wouldn't like him coming out here again either. They would probably have told him to call the police.

But he didn't want to send the police on a wild-goose chase, and part of him didn't want to be right about the pond, either. The fact that he, Lana, and Chloe discovered the first two bodies could be seen as coincidence. Finding the second set—or at least knowing where they were—might put them under suspicion.

Calling in a hunch and having it be wrong might do the same thing.

The Franklin driveway was filled with potholes from the chilly winter. One of the first things Clark's dad did every spring was repair the road. That way, he said, the equipment would remain in better shape year-round. Better to spend a few dollars up front than pay for it all later on.

Clark watched the house go past as Chloe followed the driveway between the barns. Yellow police tape held the house doors closed and the barn doors as well.

"Chloe," he said, his voice sounding loud in the quiet car, "did your source say anything about the barns?"

"No." She was frowning as she stared at the road. Her car wasn't made for these kinds of conditions, and she was obviously beginning to realize it. "Why?"

"The police tape on the barn doors," Clark said.

"I suspect this whole place is cordoned off as a crime scene," Pete said, "whether they found anything inside or not."

"Maybe." But Clark didn't like it. Maybe there was more evidence in the barns, more reasons for the police theory.

"Do you think we should check it out?" Lana asked.

"When we're done at the pond," Chloe said.

"You think we're really going to find anything there?" Pete asked.

"I hope not." The tires caught in a rut, forcing Chloe to struggle with the wheel. Clark fought the urge to reach over and help her. He'd done that once, and she'd been furious at him.

"So maybe the barn would be a good idea," Lana said.

"I want to see where this pond is first," Chloe said. "It bugs me that the police missed it."

"If they didn't mention the barns, maybe they didn't mention the pond either," Clark said.

Chloe shook her head. "I asked specifically where they'd searched. They mentioned the farm itself, which anyone would know included the barns. And they said they looked over the rest of the property. But if Clark's right and that fence looks like the area is fenced off, they might not have thought of that as property."

The car jolted again. Clark's knees hit the dashboard. The taller he got, the more he hated small cars.

The road kept going straight, leading toward the fields. But on the left side, Clark saw faint lines, indicating the old road. The lines were hidden by thick weeds and brush, but it didn't take X-ray vision to see through that. Just experience with farms and old, abandoned roads.

"Stop here," he said.

Chloe slammed on the brakes. The tires caught and held, sliding the car on the gravel. Dust rose behind them, as if they'd been caught in a horrible wind storm.

"Jeez, Chloe," Pete said. "You could've eased to a stop."

"When you have your own car, you can ease," she said, tucking a strand of hair behind her ear. She popped the door open, sending clouds of dust inside.

Clark coughed and got out, standing up so that his head rose above the dust cloud.

Pete climbed out after him. "I don't see anything."

"Wait until the dust clears," Lana said from the other side of the car.

"I always wondered where that saying came from," Clark said.

"That's not what I mean," Pete said. "I mean, I didn't see anything to make us stop."

"Me, either," Chloe said. "But Clark did, and he seems to have this X-ray vision lately, so I trust him."

Clark felt his cheeks heat up. But he didn't say anything, knowing that Chloe was just turning a phrase.

Still, it came awfully close to the bone.

The dust was settling. Down in this hollow behind the farm buildings, the air was thick and close. It also smelled faintly of loam, rotting vegetation, and stagnant water.

"I see it." Lana stepped toward the faint tracks that Clark had seen. "This was a road once, notice?"

Pete and Clark stepped around the car. Chloe was staring at the tracks.

"I wouldn't have noticed that," she said.

"Living on a farm," Clark said, "you tend to notice the land."

"Yeah, well, it's creepy down here." Pete rubbed his left arm as if it ached. "You guys came down here yesterday?"

"No," Lana said. "We were up at the top of the driveway. That's when we saw the—you know. Danny."

Pete nodded.

"It doesn't look like anyone's been down here," Chloe said. She was studying the gravel road. Her car's tracks appeared to be the only ones made recently.

"The police should have checked this out," Lana said. "It's awfully close to the house."

"But it does look unused," Pete said.

Clark shaded his eyes with his hand. From the back of the house, he had a hunch this dip in the road didn't look like much. The graveled area made it all seem like extra parking instead of an actual road.

"I think the police are more focused on finding the Franklins' truck than on searching the property," Chloe said.

"What if the rest of the family is alive somewhere?" Pete asked.

"I don't think they'd be hanging around here." Lana had walked deeper into the weeds. "These tracks go into that underbrush."

Her movements sent up a cloud of gnats. She swatted at her arms absently.

A mosquito circled Pete. He slapped at it. "Isn't it early for bugs?"

"It was the heat yesterday," Clark said. "Better hope for one more good freeze."

"You're a sick man," Pete said. "You know I hate winter."

"I thought you hated bugs more," Clark said as he walked toward Lana. She had stopped just at the edge of the underbrush.

"See?" Lana said. "I don't think anyone's been in there for a long time."

"Someone has." Chloe pointed toward a bit of material hanging off a twig. The material was green flannel, almost hidden by the buds that had come out in the warm weather.

Chloe had slung both cameras around her neck. She picked one up, and took a picture.

"I don't see how anyone got through that tangle," Pete said.

Clark pointed to a dark space, hidden in shadow. "Deer bed," he said. "There's a thin animal trail through there. That's how someone got in and out."

"We can't go that way," Chloe said. "We'll contaminate the crime scene."

"We have no idea if it is a crime scene." Lana sounded prickly, which was unusual for her.

"I can smell stagnant water," Clark said. "Can't you?"

Lana sniffed. "Brackish. Yeah, I can."

"That's where your mosquitoes came from," Chloe said to Pete.

Then she walked past all of them and ducked into the dark space that Clark had seen. Somehow she managed to avoid the flannel.

"Wow," she said, her voice sounding far away. "Shades of Middle Earth."

"What does that mean?" Pete asked.

"I'm not sure I want to know," Clark said.

"Haven't you read Tolkien?" Lana asked, ducking in the space after Chloe.

"Saw the movie," Pete whispered to Clark. "Does that count?"

"Probably not to Lana," Clark whispered back.

He started to follow when he heard Lana whistle.

"Not Middle Earth, Chloe," Lana said, her voice strangely faint. "More like *Alice's Adventures through the Looking Glass*. All we need is a giant caterpillar and a hookah pipe."

The brambles caught in Clark's hair, and something bit the bare skin on the back of his hand. It almost felt like that something spit the hunk of skin out before flying away.

Clark grinned. He didn't get bitten by bugs very often, and those that did bite him always seemed to react like they'd tasted something bad.

"I'm getting eaten alive here." Pete was just behind Clark. Even though he was smaller, he was really shaking the underbrush.

"It's your cologne," Chloe said. Her voice sounded closer now. "Didn't anyone tell you not to wear cologne in the woods?"

"I wasn't planning to crawl around in the woods when I

got up this morning," Pete said. "And it's not cologne. It's aftershave."

"Oops, sorry," Chloe said. "Forgot about the mysteries of shaving."

Clark stepped out of the bramble into an area touched with darkness. Giant mushrooms grew around the base of a nearby tree. Here the air had the smell of perpetual damp. The ground was marshy.

Chloe stood near the tree. Lana had taken a few steps farther, leaving footprints in the muck.

Pete burst out of the bramble, stumbling on a rotting log to Clark's left. "Wow," Pete said. "It almost feels like we're not in Kansas anymore."

"We have votes for Oz, Alice, and Middle Earth," Lana said. "You want to add an allusion, Clark? We're taking literary and movie-related, apparently."

But Clark didn't want to add anything. This place was making him very uncomfortable. Not because there were meteor rocks—there weren't—or anything obviously dangerous, but because it felt so isolated.

He looked at the ground, saw that the tracks were long gone. A small pile of dirt had gathered near the tree. It was probably quite cold back here in the winter, and the last of the snow might have melted only a few days ago.

That wasn't good for tracking. Neither was the marshy aspect. Lana's deep footprints were already filling with water, disappearing almost as quickly as she had made them.

"I don't see a pond," Pete said.

"That's because we're standing on the edge of it, unless I miss my guess." Chloe took one picture for good measure.

"This isn't a pond," Lana said. "This is a marsh."

"That's why they made their own pond," Clark said.

"They couldn't control the water here, and it probably got contaminated real easily."

"Besides, who would want to come here regularly?" Pete asked, and shuddered.

"It looks like it gets deeper up ahead." Chloe pointed to an area around the tree.

Clark stopped near her. His shoes were getting wet. The ground was saturated here.

"This is the perfect place to hide bodies," Chloe said. "If Mr. Franklin did kill his family, wouldn't he have hidden them here instead of the other pond?"

"Probably another point in the argument against him doing it." Lana was the farthest forward. She raised up on her toes and scanned the area in front of her. "Although I don't know how anyone could have gotten much farther in here without getting really wet himself."

"Could always clean up back at the farm," Pete said. "Was there mud inside the house?"

"Not that we could see," Chloe said.

"There's still an old pump outside," Clark said. "I used it yesterday. Anyone could have cleaned up there."

Pete nodded. "How're we going to search this?"

"We're not," Lana said. "Not without the right gear. It gets deeper just ahead of me."

"I'm going to use the telephoto," Chloe said. "Sometimes it shows me a lot."

She brought the camera to her face and adjusted the lens as if it were a telescope.

Clark walked over to Lana. He sank deeper in the muck than any of them, but he was bigger and weighed more. If anything had been thrown back here, it would have been very hard to find.

Lana kept looking, moving her head, just as Chloe was.

Clark stood next to Lana and looked, too. The sun dappled through the trees. Flies buzzed ahead, and small pools of gnats rose like they were a single creature.

A lot of the surrounding trees had rotted, and moss grew on their sides. The brackish smell was thick, but not quite overwhelming. It was an odor of the land, something that Clark had grown up with.

He could see why the Franklins never used this part of the land, and why the map showed it fenced off. He had a hunch the fence had rotted away long ago. The land was too saturated to use as farmland. There was probably a creek nearby, close enough to feed this marshland—or perhaps there were underground springs.

Whatever caused the water to seep through the ground like this must have made this area hell in the summer, with the heat, the smell, and the bugs.

"I think I see some flannel up there." Chloe pointed toward an old oak that looked like it had been split by lightning a generation ago. She kept her camera to her face, then adjusted the lens. "I'm pretty sure."

"Let me see," Lana said, reaching for the camera. Chloe handed it to her, and Lana put it up to her eyes.

Clark couldn't see anything from this distance. But he would be able to see in the water.

He used his X-ray vision, scanning first the water ahead of them, and then moving toward the split oak, little bit by little bit.

The marsh was deeper than he expected, and filled with tiny bones, most of them from birds or animals that had gotten caught in the water, or perhaps prey that had gotten eaten there. Little pointed skulls, from some kind of rodent, littered one entire section like someone was keeping a collection of them. But the skulls were scattered enough that he knew the collection was an animal's not a human's.

When he got to the split oak, the water grew even

deeper. The tiny bones he'd seen closer in were missing here, as if this was too deep even for the animals to mess with.

"I think I see something," Pete said. He was crouching, looking through the underbrush. Everyone turned in the direction he was pointing.

Another ripped piece of flannel and broken branches, a lot of them. The breaks looked pretty recent.

"Do you think it's shallower over there?" Chloe asked.

Lana brought the camera down. "You'd either have to test it or have local knowledge."

"I wouldn't want to test anything in this place," Pete said.

Clark scanned that area with his special vision and saw nothing as well. He returned his gaze to the oak, looking at the area around it. It took a moment for his eyes to re-adjust to the X-ray vision, but when they did, he saw what he had missed before.

Two hands, entwined, caught in weeds along the bottom. The hands were attached to arms, but Clark couldn't see how far they went, or if there was an actual body behind them.

"Well, Eagle Eyes," Chloe said to him. "Do you see anything?"

"I don't know," he said. "Can I have the camera?"

Lana handed it to him. Clark put the camera to his eyes, and adjusted the lens. It did work like a telescope. The oak tree was much clearer. He could even see the damaged bark.

Something clung to that bark—not just flannel, but strands of brown hair, too long to belong to anything but a human being. And, near the tree's roots, a footprint big enough to be his own.

"Yeah," Clark said. "Some hair near that flannel, and a print near the base of the tree."

Pete slapped his arm and everyone jumped, looking at him in surprise. "I told you," he said. "I'm getting eaten alive back here."

Chloe took the camera from Clark and looked where he'd been looking.

Pete slapped his arm again.

"And," Clark said, not sure how much he should stretch the truth. "I thought I saw something else."

"What?" Chloe was adjusting the lens. "I see the hair—it's really fine. Nice work, Clark."

"Near the print. See that thing along the edge of the water? Is that a sleeve?"

He knew there were some leaves floating along the surface. He hoped she would misread one.

"It could be," she said.

Lana looked up at him, her eyes wide. "Are you going to check it out again, Clark?"

"In that water?" Pete said. "He'd have to shower for a week to start smelling like a person again."

Clark blessed him silently. "The last time, I went in because I had the mistaken thought that Danny was alive. I don't see any reason to go in this time."

Chloe took a few shots, then eased the camera down, holding it in one hand. "Especially since the police aren't going to be happy with us coming here today."

"Even though we might have found something."

"Especially if we found something," Chloe said. "Discovering another body? Or two? Or three? That's going to look somewhat suspicious."

"You're not suggesting we just leave, are you?" Lana asked.

Chloe shook her head. "Not at all. I'm just warning you

all that this is going to get ugly if there truly is someone there."

Pete slapped his arm a third time. "Well, can we make our decision near the car? I'm not enjoying providing dinner for a whole host of baby mosquitoes."

"That's mama mosquitoes," Lana said.

"I don't really care," Pete said. "I'm getting welts."

"My phone's back at the car," Chloe said. "I'm going to get a few more pictures. You want to call the authorities, Pete?"

"You mind if I crawl inside and close the doors and windows while I do it?"

Chloe gave him an absent smile. "Not at all."

"Then I'm all for calling the authorities." Pete slipped back through the brambles. As he went through, he cursed once, then cried "ouch!" followed by another slapping sound.

"I'll go help him," Lana said. "There's nothing more we can do here."

Clark stayed while Chloe took even more pictures. He walked along the edge of the deeper water, using his special vision to see if he could see more of the bodies. He had nearly reached the section where the other flannel was when he could see farther.

The arms were attached to two bodies. He'd been half-hoping that the arms were remains washed into the marsh from an old graveyard or something. But the bones didn't look old, not like some of the animal bones.

And these bodies were entwined together, almost as if they'd been wrapped together. Too deep to be seen from the surface.

Clark hoped his lie would hold—at least well enough for the police to bring in divers.

And, at the same time, he hoped he was wrong about the

newness of the corpses. Because if they had been dumped here recently, then he was looking at at least two more Franklins.

The rest of the family might have been hidden in this marsh. Only with the help of the police would anyone know for sure.

CHAPTER TEN

So far, this day had been one of the worst of Lionel Luthor's life—and it looked like it had just gotten worse.

Luthor was tied even more tightly to the chair than he had been before. That morning, he had taken advantage of his captor's shower and managed to slide his chair toward the kitchen. With the give in his ropes, Luthor figured he could find something sharp in there and cut the ropes off.

But he hadn't counted on the uneven flooring. Just as he reached the middle part of the room, one of the chair legs hit a raised floorboard. The chair toppled precariously for a moment, then fell to its side.

Without his hands free, there was no way he could break the fall. He landed, hard, on his left elbow. The cracking sound he heard and the pain shooting up his arm probably had nothing to do with the cheapness of the rotting wood flooring.

The sound of his fall reverberated through the entire place, and the shower shut off. No matter how hard Luthor tried, he couldn't get his chair upright again.

Still, his captor's reaction when he stumbled out of the bathroom, hastily pulling a pair of pants over his wet frame, was "Oh, crap, Mr. Luthor. We can't let them catch you like this."

Them, as if *they* were someone other than this scrawny captor with his beady eyes, two-day growth of beard, and nervous tics. Luthor figured this guy was the dumb one, the cousin or the brother who had thought he was going along for a good time and a lot of beer, and instead got stuck with all the heavy work.

The man managed to pull Luthor's chair upright—this captor was amazingly strong for such a scrawny man—but he was shaking as he did so.

"Mr. Luthor, you don't understand what you're dealing with. This isn't some movie. You get outta here, and you'll just get lost outside. Then they'll shoot you. Better to stay put, hope that your son comes up with the money, and then we can all go home."

Luthor let him talk, hoping the man would say something a bit more revealing, but he never did. Over the space of the day, they did come up with a rhythm of sorts.

When it became clear that something had snapped in Luthor's arm—the swelling and bruising told them that much—the man decided he could untie that hand. As a result, Luthor was able to feed himself—awkwardly (the arm was truly injured)—and drink liquids.

He was also able to use the facilities—with the man tying his good arm up to a towel rack first. Luthor tried and was unable to untie the hand with his injured arm. Reaching across his stomach to the tied hand was one of the most painful things Luthor had ever done in his life. Still, he did his best, and nearly passed out as a result.

His captor spent most of the afternoon monitoring a computer in the back room, and not speaking a lot. Luthor heard the warning bells, the sound of fingers against keys, and an occasional curse, but little more.

Luthor had just been about to see if he could talk his captor into some sort of lenient treatment—something that might give Luthor an advantage—when he heard the sound of tires on gravel. Through the windows in front of him, he saw a large truck pull up outside.

The truck had once been red, but had faded in the harsh Kansas weather to a dirty rust. Dents on the side of the bed showed that the truck had been heavily used.

As the truck wheeled to a stop, Luthor realized that he hadn't seen the limo. He wondered what they had done with it. These captors were smarter than he originally thought. They knew the limo would give them away, and they hadn't kept it nearby.

His captor came out of the back room, saw the truck, and actually turned pale. Luthor thought that was interesting. He had employees who were afraid of him, but they only had that reaction when they had done something wrong.

Had this man done something he shouldn't have?

Luthor didn't want to contemplate it.

His captor came closer and put his hands on Luthor's shoulders. The gesture was both comforting and menacing at the same time. Luthor wasn't used to someone in his personal space, but the man's grip was light, almost friendly.

"Mr. Luthor, these guys here, they're not nice men. Don't piss them off, whatever you do. They still haven't decided what to do with you after the money comes. They're pretty—"

Footsteps on the porch made his captor shut up and back away. The hands left Luthor's shoulders, and a chill ran down his spine.

When the door opened, letting in sunlight and the smell of new spring grass, Luthor made himself breathe easily. This could all be a game they were playing to make him reveal something.

Well, he knew game theory better than anyone, and he wasn't going to play by their rules. He was going to invent his own.

The two men who came in the door looked familiar in that same archetypal way that the first captor did. Luthor wasn't sure if he'd actually seen them before, or if they were just the standard rednecks from central casting.

These two seemed even more true to type than his captor.

They were large, square, and solid. They had full beards that hid most of their features, and they wore John Deere hats pulled halfway down their foreheads. All he could see were eyes, surrounded by sun-reddened skin. Blue eyes, watery, and yet full of menace.

The first time he saw the leader's eyes and their malicious intent was the first time Luthor truly believed he might not make it out of this situation alive.

"Look how the mighty hath fallen," said the second man as he stomped into the room. His boots left more dried mud on the hardwood floor.

The first man remained silent, his gaze never leaving Luthor's face.

"Don't got nothing to say for yourself, Lionel?" the second man said.

"I'm not one for pleading," Luthor said, "and I doubt a polite request to leave will get me anywhere."

"You got it in one." The second man laughed. He walked away from the door, heading into the kitchen, and opened the refrigerator, pulling out a can of beer.

Luthor's original captor watched this with more trepidation than Luthor felt. "How'd it go?" his captor asked the first man.

The man finally broke his gaze away from Luthor's. Luthor felt its loss like the loss of a physical presence. "Dunno. That's up to the kid."

"I hear the kid hates his dad," the captor said.

"That true, Lionel? Can't even get your own kid to warm up to you?" The second man grabbed a chair, pulled it over, and sat down, legs spread. He clutched the beer in his left hand.

"What does Lex have to do with this?" Luthor asked, even though he had a hunch. He simply figured the more he could get these people to speak to him, the better chance he had of understanding them. The better he understood them, the easier it would be to play them.

If the ache and swelling in his arm, and the headache they were creating didn't interfere with his powers of concentration too badly.

"Only everything." The first man spoke for the first time, and Luthor recognized the voice from the limo. The one he'd thought didn't sound as educated as one of the others. Was his captor the educated one then? Or was it all an act?

"Think the kid cares enough to pay for you?" the second man said. "Because if he don't, we're all screwed."

"No, we're not." The first man cuffed his partner's head hard enough to dislodge his John Deere hat. The hat tumbled into his partner's lap, and as he bent forward, Luthor noted that he was balding on top. Not as young then as Luthor had initially thought.

Luthor waited in silence. He wanted to know how they wouldn't be screwed if Lex failed to pay the ransom.

"C'mon. I thought this was about the cash," the second man said.

"It's about revenge." Luthor's captor spoke from behind him. It almost felt like his captor was watching his back, but that couldn't be. There was a dynamic here that Luthor didn't entirely understand.

He felt that dynamic was the key to his survival. He would watch, listen, and work it out.

"Revenge?" he asked. "For what?"

"For everything, Lionel. You do so much crap to people you forget everything you done." The second man took another sip of his beer. Then he put the cap back over his bald spot. "See, if you was just a bad man instead of a truly evil old fart, you'd have an idea what's got us so riled up. But you've done so much horrible stuff over the years, we could be getting you back for any old thing. In fact, I think it's better you don't know. You can imagine lots worse stuff than we can ever come up with."

That was probably true—at least of the second man. He didn't look like someone with a lot of imagination. But that first man, the man of few words, the obvious leader, he seemed to have imagination to spare.

"What've we got so far?" Luthor's captor asked. "Any word?"

"Not from LuthorCorp, directly." The first man took a root beer out of the refrigerator. No hope then that they'd all get drunk and stupid. The first man wasn't going to allow that.

"What about indirectly?" Luthor's captor asked. He sounded eager. Maybe he wasn't as nice a guy as Luthor had initially thought.

The first man smiled. It was a slow, cold smile. "Stock's down ten points, and still plummeting. Seems the entire country thinks LuthorCorp can't survive without you, Mr. Luthor."

Stock spirals happened. If Luthor got free, the stocks would recover. If he didn't, and the first man's analysis was right, then everything Luthor had worked for his entire life would be lost, lost because he was.

He didn't let his dismay over that show on his face. If there was one thing he learned in the field of business, it was how to keep his emotions off his face.

"So," said Number Two. "Tell us about your kid."

"What do you want to know?" Luthor asked.

"How come he hasn't responded to our note yet."

"I trust you gave him a way to respond," Luthor said, careful to keep the hope out of his voice. If they had given Lex a way to respond, then there would be a way to trace these miscreants. The day would be simply that, a bad day, easily forgotten.

"Not directly." Number One smiled. He had a chipped bottom tooth, right up front. His teeth were coffee-stained, the chip worst of all.

"Then how can you be certain he hasn't responded?" Luthor said.

"No financial activity in the accounts," Number Two said. "He should be gathering the funds now."

Luthor's stomach clenched. "Well, it sounds to me as if you've made getting funds difficult for him. You know most corporations don't have a lot of cash reserves, and our lines of credit are tied to our stock price."

"English, Lionel. Speakee English," Number Two said.

"He is," said Luthor's captor. "He's saying that you screwed yourself."

"We screwed ourselves, friend," Number One said, and in that moment, Luthor knew that they were smarter than he had originally given them credit for. *Friend.* They weren't going to slip and admit names.

Although it did bother him that they allowed him to see their faces. That didn't bode well for him. Perhaps they didn't want him to know names because they were going to let him talk to Lex on the phone, and perhaps they didn't care if he saw who they were because they planned to kill him once they had the money.

That's what he would do if he decided to stoop to something as mindless as kidnapping.

"You think that makes sense?" Number One was asking Luthor's captor.

His captor shrugged. "Big business isn't my forte."

"Well, money's money, and you can't tell me that one of the largest corporations in the world doesn't got enough assets to cover ten million in cash."

Luthor's throat tightened. Ten million? They were only asking ten million for him? And then he felt a faint amusement at himself, worrying how much criminals—criminals who just admitted they had no idea about big business—thought he was worth.

"You sure that kid of yours'll come through?" Number Two asked again.

Luthor realized he hadn't answered the question, and not because he was dodging it. He truly didn't know the answer.

He had no idea what Lex would do.

He would hope that Lex would use all the resources at his fingertips—and Luthor had left him with a lot of resources—to find this place, rescue him, and take care of these three men. Luthor also hoped that Lex was savvy enough to pretend to play their games.

But Lex was becoming more and more of a mystery. He wasn't making the mistakes that he used to, and he was thinking more on his own.

The thoughts he had unnerved Luthor. Lex had tested off the charts in intelligence and, it seemed to Luthor, never used that brainpower, until recently. Someday Lex would realize that he was smarter than his father, smarter than everyone around him, and he would take advantage of that.

The conversation they'd had a few weeks ago suddenly floated through Luthor's mind. He could actually hear Lex's voice in his head:

You know what those emperors you're so fond of talking about were really afraid of? That their own sons would become successful and return to Rome at the head of their own armies.

When Luthor had queried him about that, asking if Lex was going to come to Metropolis with his own army, Lex had dodged the question.

Now he didn't need an army. All he had to do was sit on

his hands, wait, and his dad's head would be delivered to him on a silver platter.

Perhaps literally.

Luthor shuddered. The day had definitely grown worse.

It took the sheriff's office an hour to arrive, and then it was only one car, unmarked. Clark felt nervous watching it come down the driveway, kicking up dust as it weaved its way toward them.

The four of them were leaning against Chloe's car as they waited. Lana had made a second call just to make sure someone was coming, and she'd been about to make a third, when they'd heard the car's wheels squeal around the gate in front of the house.

The single car bothered all of them, and without speaking to each other, they gathered next to each other for support.

"This is the police, right?" Pete asked.

"Anyone with the right technology can listen in on cell phones," Chloe said.

"What does that mean?" Lana asked.

"It means Chloe isn't sure," Clark said. "But I am. That's deputy Roberts driving."

Deputy Roberts had arrived at yesterday's scene. He hadn't treated them well, but he had, once he realized the seriousness of the situation, handled the crime scene as well as possible.

Another man sat in the car with him. As the car fishtailed its way down the hill, Pete stood up.

"I've watched too much TV," he said.

"What does that mean?" Chloe asked.

"It means I'm not willing to believe these guys are good guys just because they're police. Shouldn't we have some kind of contingency plan? I mean, what if they did the killing?"

"Why?" Lana asked. "What reason would they have for killing Danny and Betty?"

Pete shrugged. "That's why they call these kinds of cases a mystery."

"We'll be all right," Clark said, but he was braced as well. He didn't think Roberts was involved in anything illegal, but now that Pete had put that thought in Clark's head, Clark was not going to let anyone harm his friends.

"Oh, yeah?" Pete said. "They got guns. We don't."

"If they did this, they're not going to use guns," Chloe said. "Danny and Betty were strangled."

"The police didn't do anything," Lana said. "You guys are just paranoid."

The sheriff's car skidded to a stop in front of them. The dust cloud continued forward, enveloping them in dirty brown air for the second time that afternoon. Clark's eyes stung. Next to him, Lana coughed and Pete made spitting sounds. Only Chloe remained quiet.

The car doors opened and slammed shut. It took a moment for Clark to be able to see clearly. Roberts and his partner, the same man who had spoken to them the day before, whose name they had not gotten, walked toward them.

"You guys just like hanging out down here or you got some kind of agenda?" Roberts asked.

"We're friends of Danny's," Lana said.

"Strange way you got of showing it. Snooping around where you don't belong."

The partner hung back and watched. Both men were in street clothes again.

"Did you check out the marsh?" Chloe asked.

"Why?" Roberts asked.

"Because if you did," Clark said, "we bothered you for no

reason. But if you didn't, there's something down there you might want to see."

"Something you kids put there?"

"No," Pete said, sounding very perturbed. "We're being good citizens here. What's your problem?"

The partner stepped forward, putting a hand on Roberts's arm. "We're not used to young people taking an active interest in an investigation."

"We're not used to losing friends," Lana said.

The partner's mouth twitched, and Clark could have sworn the man was suppressing a smile. "Well, then—"

"I'll take it, Davies." Roberts took one step closer to them. He seemed to be trying to intimidate them. It wasn't working with Clark.

But Roberts didn't stop in front of Clark. He stopped in front of Chloe. "I didn't appreciate those pictures in the *Torch*. We need your film for the investigation."

"I didn't use film," Chloe said. "The pictures are digital. You want me to e-mail them to you?"

"Listen, young lady, you're already in trouble for being at this crime scene. You don't want to compound it."

"She's a reporter," Clark said. "She's doing her job."

"She's a high school student," Roberts said, "and she's butting in."

"Without her, you wouldn't even have a case," Pete said. "Her and Lana and Clark. And they're doing your work for you. Stop blustering and listen to them. We saw something in that marsh. You guys need to check it out."

Roberts's mouth thinned. He obviously didn't appreciate the criticism. But Davies stepped beside him, clearly taking over this part of the investigation.

"How'd you know there was a marsh there?" he asked.

"There's an old plat map in the *Torch* office," Clark said. "I was looking at it, and saw a pond marked on it and a fence line. We figured most people wouldn't have thought it was part of the Franklin property—"

"And we couldn't remember seeing any other pond or fence for that matter," Chloe said. "We thought if we missed it, you might have."

"So you came to investigate yourselves," Roberts said. "You coulda called it in."

"Look how long it took you to respond to our call today," Lana snapped. Clark looked down at her in surprise. She had color in both cheeks. She was angry at the treatment the group was getting. "Imagine how you would have responded if we had asked you to look at the marsh without knowing if there was anything to our hunch."

Roberts's gaze flattened, but this time, Davies smiled. "Point and set to the lady. You convinced me. Now someone show me this stuff you found."

"I'll do it." Chloe led him toward the dark opening in the bramble.

"I'll go with you," Clark said. He wasn't going to let Chloe go alone with anyone into that area, not after the little speech Pete gave. It was just enough to make Clark extra cautious—and a little paranoid.

He stumbled under the brambles, felt the gnats attack again, and then the brackish stench of standing water hit him. Chloe and Davies were already standing at the edge of the marsh, Chloe pointing at the split oak tree.

Davies was taking her seriously. He used the telephoto lens she offered him and looked at the bits of fabric. He didn't see any body, of course, or the fingers Clark had mentioned, but that didn't matter.

As he handed the camera back to Chloe, Davies said, "We should've checked this out yesterday. I even came down here. I had no idea that this was more than an uncrossable thicket. We'll radio for some divers."

Clark shuddered at the idea of going into the water, but he knew it was their job. He just wished they'd hurry up about it. He didn't like being the only one with the knowledge that there were at least two more bodies in that marsh.

And he wanted to find out who they were.

CHAPTER ELEVEN

In a tiny room behind the Club Noir in one of the seedier neighborhoods of Metropolis, Lex stood, his hands behind his back. He'd been cautioned years ago not to touch anything in here, and he never had.

The room had fluorescent overhead lights, which he had never seen on. Instead, most of the light came from a dozen computer screens of various shapes and sizes. Over one desk, a small halogen lamp burned.

The stale air smelled of Cheetos and mochacinos, along with the faint scents of alcohol, perfume, and cigarettes filtering in from the club. Three teenage boys whom Lex only knew by their screen monikers—DeadMan, Terror, and Aces—sat with their backs to each other, their fingers working the keyboards.

An old schoolmate, whose real name Lex had vowed not to repeat, sat at the largest screen working the digital images. He was a year older than Lex and had dropped out of boarding school when the FBI came after him for hacking. His real name, Phil Brodsky, didn't have the menace it should have.

Brodsky could open any file, find any piece of information, dig through any encoded system he happened to stumble across.

And he stumbled across a lot of them.

Lex liked keeping him around. Brodsky had taught Lex everything he knew about computer hacking and then some, but Lex didn't have the natural talent for it that Brodsky did. Brodsky was almost an idiot savant. It was as if he became the code.

Lex had to think his way through each and every piece of it. Hacking, while logical, was too much like homework for him. Lex preferred to work with people, to get them to reveal their weaknesses, instead of finding those weaknesses hidden in some obscure part of the Internet.

"Not very sophisticated really," Terror said. He'd been assigned to trace the e-mail. The other two kids were working on the video images and the photographs.

Brodsky had the tough task. He was going through the security tape, frame by frame, searching for something, anything that would help Lex find his father.

"They used *A Luddite's Guide to Computer Hacking*. It's pretty clear." Terror leaned back and cracked his knuckles. He was the one who lived on Cheetos. The orange stains on his fingertips appeared to be permanent.

"You mean *An Idiot's Guide*?" Lex asked.

"Nope," Terror said. "I mean *A Luddite's Guide*."

"Would modern Luddites even know what that word means?" Lex asked.

"Not if they were, like, you know, our age. But if they're old," DeadMan said. "Those kinda books usually appeal to old guys anyway. Most guys who really want to do this stuff, they learn by doing, you know."

"And they're computer oriented," Lex said, "so they download their information."

"Exactamundo, dude," DeadMan said.

Of Brodsky's three sidekicks, DeadMan was the one Lex liked the least. He wasn't as talented as the other two, and he always had a chip on his shoulder when Lex appeared. Lex knew that DeadMan was posturing, putting on the hacker persona straight out of Hollywood, but Lex also knew that DeadMan didn't have enough of a personality to hide behind the persona.

"This *Luddite's Guide*," Lex said, "it actually lays out how to send an untraceable e-mail?"

"In 1999 terms," Aces said. His fingers continued to move across the keys as he spoke. He had taken a single digital image and refined it, so that now he was looking at a tiny section of it. Lex was too far away to know what it was a section of.

"How different is it now?" Lex asked.

"There's a million better ways to do it," Terror said. "This one is so by the book. I mean, I could trace it with my eyes closed now."

"Put it this way," Aces said. "No one does it this way anymore."

"When it hits print, man, it is so beyond passé that it's like Henry Ford material." DeadMan stood, tossed his paper Starbucks cup over Lex's head, and missed the wastebasket. He didn't go over and pick up the cup.

Neither did Lex, although he was tempted. He preferred the world neat.

"So where did this e-mail originate?" Lex asked.

"Metropolis," Terror said.

Lex had expected that. He would have been surprised if the e-mail had originated anywhere else.

"Where, exactly, in Metropolis?" Lex asked.

"An Internet café about five blocks from here. I know the guy who runs it. We got a time code on the e-mail. He might remember who sent it."

Lex doubted that the owner would remember, but it was a start. "Give me the information. I'll send one of my people."

"No offense, Lex," Brodsky said, "but he won't talk to one of your 'people.'"

"I'll go then," Lex said.

"No need," Terror said. "I already e-mailed him. I expect a response any minute now."

Lex shouldn't have been surprised at the swiftness of all of this—after all, he was raised in a computer-driven world—but he never sank deeply into the lifestyle. He wished they hadn't e-mailed. He wanted to see the guy's eyes, know if he was lying, if he'd sent it himself, if he was covering up.

But right now, Lex would take what he could get.

"What about the fax?" Lex asked.

"Tougher," Aces said. "Shoulda brought us to your dad's office, let us work with the machine."

"Some things even I can't do," Lex said. Or wouldn't do, for fear that his father might come back in the middle of everything and not understand the measures Lex was taking.

Then there was Lex's smaller fear, the one he hadn't voiced to anyone, that his father was somehow involved in the kidnapping, that it was a ploy to test Lex (and if he ever discovered that, he'd quit trying to rescue his father right then and there) or that it was designed to shake up the market a little, find out how the market would respond if something happened to Lionel Luthor.

Lex liked to think his father wasn't that devious, but he'd be lying to himself. His father was that devious. So far, though, Lex couldn't find an obvious reason to fake a kidnapping.

"I know, bro," Aces said. He had a smaller window on his screen, running code. On the main portion, he continued manipulating the digital image he'd been working on for the past fifteen minutes. "Had to hack into the phone company. Your dad's office is tight."

"He means that in a good way," Brodsky said. "The phone company's easier."

"Way easier, dude," said DeadMan, in a tone that let Lex know that they'd tried to break into LuthorCorp before.

DeadMan was trying to get a rise out of him, so Lex ignored him.

"And?" Lex asked. "What's the phone company tell you?"

"Fax came from a copy shop on the other side of Metropolis, a good five, six miles from the Internet café. And the fax came in at the same time as your e-mail."

"The copy shop could have sent the fax at a prescribed time, right?" Lex asked.

"Doubtful," Aces said. "The shop would've left its coding on the fax. Didn't do that."

"How hard is it to wipe off the sending number?" Lex asked.

"Not that tough if you've got a manual. Tougher if you don't. And weird in a place like that, where the code's damn near hardwired in. You got a real technogeek on your hands, Lex," Aces said.

"Two of them, I think," Brodsky said. "At least."

Three. This merely confirmed what the security tape showed. Two men working the technological corridors of Metropolis this morning, and one man (person?) guarding his father. At least that would be how Lex would do it.

But Lex knew how treacherous his father was. He'd have someone keeping an eye on the old man all the time. Most people underestimated Lionel Luthor, thinking him a crude bully.

Lex would never make that mistake.

Although there was yet another option. All three players were in Metropolis, sending out video e-mails and hidden faxes, while his father lay dead in a ditch somewhere.

A computer pinged.

"Got an answer," Terror said. "With pictures. Come look."

Lex stepped closer to Terror's machine. Terror's e-mail

ities. Stories about the effects of meteor rocks, emus plants, and mad scientists might be better served internship at one of the checkout stand tabloids in-f a respected paper like the *Planet.*

the sadness—and much of her drive to cover this -was coming from her friendship (if she could call it vith Danny. He'd been a nice guy, and she'd noticed was having a tough time lately.

just hadn't done anything about it. She hadn't even d the story of Mr. Franklin's layoff like Danny asked The conversation played over and over in her mind tried and mostly failed to sleep the night before.

ny, I'm sorry that your dad got laid off. But this stuff ıs. It's business news, but not the kind of thing the covers. I mean, we'll put an article in, but it won't be

e, employees were targeted for this. Not just my dad, er people, people who had finally gotten a second —

sorry, Danny. People get laid off all the time. I don't sound harsh, but it's not really news.

she'd meant was that it wasn't really news to her. It ake her pulse pound and her fingers move across the he wasn't going to be a reporter so that she could ity Council meetings and layoffs and other ever-hat hit the newspaper as seasonally as Christmas ing.

e she should have listened to Danny, though. He had angle on the layoffs, and she had ignored it. Maybe d talked to Danny's father, things might have gone ly. Or maybe, if she had listened, she might have omething else, something that would have given wenty-four hours some meaning.

rst diver's head popped out of the water. He had

program was open. An e-mail from the Internet café filled the preview window, with an attachment indicated.

The e-mail started with no salutation or preamble, as if the two men had been carrying on a conversation instead of writing letters to each other.

```
Your guy's a weird dude. Worried me, so
took a couple pictures from a few different
angles. Got mostly nose hairs on the
computer's cam, but got some good ones when
he paid. Take a look. Wouldn'ta even
thought he knew what e-mail was. Guess it
takes all kinds. Tell your buddy no one's
used the keyboard since. I'll detach, put
on a new one. I don't want any obvious Feds
in here, but I'll hand it over to a
nonobvious one. Lemme know.
```

"That's kind of him," Lex said, wondering what was in it for the café owner. Did he expect a payout?

"Dude, he's not being kind. He just doesn't want trouble, and he understands chain of evidence because he's had some experience with it, if you know what I mean." DeadMan had whirled his chair around and was staring at Lex pointedly.

"I suspect we've all had experience with chain of evidence," Lex said, feeling a bit defensive. If they wanted to compare arrest records, let them try. He'd have them all beat. Conviction records were another matter. They didn't have fathers with friends on the force.

Fathers with influence.

Fathers who might be dead.

Lex crouched behind Terror's chair. He was getting tired of standing. Being awake for more than thirty-six hours was beginning to take its toll.

"Let's see what your friend considers a weird dude," he said.

Terror opened the attachments. The first few were too close to be valuable, just like the café owner warned. If a man could be identified by a single eyebrow and a few open pores, then maybe Lex could've used them. But there wasn't enough information there to help.

The other photographs, taken at the desk, were of a broad-shouldered man who wore a John Deere cap and a beard that might or might not have been fake. His flannel shirt, obviously dirty blue jeans, and work boots marked him as someone who didn't come to Metropolis often.

"Whoa," DeadMan said, doing a respectable Keanu Reeves imitation. "Redneck alert."

"No wonder he didn't want this guy in there," Aces said, looking over Terror's shoulder.

"Why?" Lex asked.

"Scare off the regulars. You gotta figure if this guy knows enough about computers to send e-mail, he's not writing to Granny. He's doing a Timothy McVeigh or something. Not something any respectable café wants to be involved in," Terror said.

"Are you saying that if he'd come in looking like one of you guys, no one would've noticed?" Lex asked.

"Damned straight," DeadMan said. "You don't get farmers in places like that unless they don't want their minister to figure out what they're doing. It's either bombs or kiddie porn, neither of which is good for some café's future."

Lex nodded. He stood up. His knees cracked. "This is a good start, then. Can you print up some of those pictures?"

"Doing it now," Terror said. "Figured you'd want them."

"And there's no coding on our stuff either," Brodsky said. "So your FBI buddies aren't going to find anything here."

"They aren't even going to look t
"Why do you think I came to you in th
Brodsky nodded. "Give me another h
the images analyzed. I'm sure we'll ha
for you by then."
Lex took the pictures Terror offered
got so far is good. Tell your friend at th
a plainclothes FBI guy. He'll show a
Maybe the fingerprints'll tell us someth
"If the guy's got a record," Brodsky s
"As smooth as this operation's been
"I'd be surprised if he didn't."

Chloe could have kissed Pete. He v
wonderful, very supportive, and helpful
Detective Roberts's attention away fro
arrived, so that she was able to sneak
and photograph them working.
She'd already gotten several good
into the murky water, and coming o
shoes were full of water, she had muc
her feet were freezing while the rest
she didn't care. She was getting mor
By the time she got done with the
actually have a clipping file big en
Planet for that summer internship t
She slapped absently at a mosqu
go down in the water again. She f
the internship in connection with t
dealing with Smallville's weirder
sense of obligation mixed with sad
She also knew it didn't hold th

por
Nic
for
stea
F
sto
tha
tha
S
cov
her
as
hap
Tor
muc
C
but
char
I'r
mear
W
didn'
keys.
cover
greens
advert
May
a huma
if she
differe
learned
the last
The

some kind of weed draped over his diving mask. He didn't even seem to notice. He gestured at the second diver, then went back down.

"They got anything?" Clark had come up behind her. Chloe didn't jump—she had more self-control than that—but her heart rate increased. He had the ability to move as silently as a cat.

"I don't know," she said. "They just went under again. This time it seemed urgent."

Clark nodded. He seemed subdued. Maybe it was because Lana was so heartbroken. Chloe had never realized how close Lana was with Danny; apparently Clark hadn't either.

Chloe glanced over her shoulder, but couldn't see around the tangle that marked the entrance to the marsh. Lana was out there with Pete, talking to Detective Davies. Detective Roberts was near the divers, looking annoyed.

"What is it?" Clark asked.

"You know," Chloe said slowly, "Danny said something to me last week that I kind of ignored. Now I wish I hadn't."

"What's that?"

"He was talking about the layoffs. He said certain people were targeted, and they lost their second chance."

"Like his dad?" Clark asked.

Chloe frowned. "That's what I thought when he mentioned it, and I felt bad for him, but I knew there wasn't anything I could do. I mean, we've all seen it. The layoffs, the changes. When LuthorCorp first came in and shut down the creamed corn factory, we saw a lot of people lose their jobs then."

Clark moved his palm up and down, in a kind of "be-quiet" gesture. "Pete's never really gotten over that. His parents had some kind of agreement with LuthorCorp that when they sold the factory, the employees would get to keep their jobs."

Chloe nodded. "I remember. And if I didn't, Pete would remind me of it often enough. But LuthorCorp set up a whole new factory, so the agreement didn't apply."

"You think that's what Danny was referring to?"

"No," Chloe said. "I've been thinking about it all day. Danny grew up here, like the rest of us. And I know this was personal for him, but he never came to me with a story idea before. It was like there was something else going on, something that had him worried."

"About the layoffs." Clark sighed and looked past her, staring at the spot where the divers had gone down. She doubted that he was really looking there. He seemed to be seeing something beyond all of them.

"What?" she asked.

"Lex," he said. "He didn't want the layoffs either. They came from his father, and Lex got pretty steamed about it. He said that if his dad wanted him to run the factory, then he should let him run it his way."

"That wasn't the first time that his father interfered," Chloe said.

"No," Clark said. "And each time it's had to do with employee relations."

Both divers popped to the surface again. One of them swam toward the oak. The marsh had to be very deep there. Chloe was glad she hadn't followed her instinct and tried to walk over there. More than her feet would have gotten wet.

The diver spoke to Roberts, who nodded throughout the whole conversation.

"I'd talk to Lex if I could, but this thing with his dad is going on," Clark said.

"Have you called Lex in Metropolis?"

Clark shook his head. "I imagine he's got enough to do without his friends calling him every fifteen minutes. I left a message on his voice mail, letting him know he can call if he needs to, but I doubt he will."

"Even if he does, you don't want to ask him about the layoffs in the middle of this personal crisis." Chloe knew Clark well enough to know he felt that way. She would have no qualms about it, but she was short on tact anyway.

It was, she hoped, one of the things that would make her a good reporter.

"Don't you think it's odd," Clark said slowly, "that Lex's dad is kidnapped the same day that we discover Danny's body?"

"No." Chloe didn't even need time to consider the idea. "Crime goes on all the time, Clark. What's unusual about this is that we just happened to know the people involved."

"I suppose." He didn't sound convinced. "I thought you were the person who didn't believe in coincidences."

"On the same case," Chloe said. "This is clearly not the same."

"I thought we didn't know what this was," Clark said.

Chloe bit her lower lip. She had said that, or something similar to it.

But she was saved from saying any more. The divers came out of the water, carrying something between them. She grabbed her camera and zoomed the telephoto lens on the scene by the oak tree.

The divers were carrying a body—a woman's body. Chloe could tell by the long hair hanging down. The body was covered in a brownish muck.

"It's Bonnie," Clark said.

Chloe wondered how he could tell. He was just as far away as she was, and he didn't have the benefit of the telephoto lens.

But he was right. She knew he was right the moment he

said that. Bonnie's profile came into focus, her face pale in repose.

Chloe snapped photographs, stunned that she had almost forgotten to do so. But this case had unsettled her from the first. She got some fairly good pictures of the divers bringing the body ashore, and she hoped that Roberts wouldn't confiscate her film.

She'd have to find a place to hide it before he came back over here.

Almost as if he heard her thoughts, Roberts looked in her direction. He still seemed suspicious of the three of them. Chloe was glad Lana was still by the car. She would be upset at Bonnie's death and at the fact that Roberts was blaming them.

The divers set the body down and went back into the water.

"Oh, God," Chloe said. "There's more?"

"Maybe the whole family," Clark said softly.

"And to think all of Smallville's been blaming Jed Franklin." Chloe shook her head. She brought the camera down for a moment. "He might be there with the rest of his family."

"We don't know anything yet, Chloe."

"I know," she said. "The more that happens, the less confident I feel about what we do know."

Roberts was crouching near the medical examiner, who had come out with the divers. They were leaning over the body, and they seemed even more distressed than they had been the day before.

"I wonder what's going on," Chloe said.

"I could slog over there and find out," Clark said.

She shook her head. "We'll learn soon enough."

Clark gave her a sharp look. "That's not like you, Chloe."

She shrugged. "I don't have the stomach for this one, I guess."

He got that familiar studious look he had so often, as if he could see deep down inside her. "I would think this story would fire you up more than the others."

"What do you mean?" she asked.

"You knew everyone, and there's a mystery here. You've been at the crime scene twice. This is your story, not anyone else's. You've even scooped The *Daily Planet*."

"They don't usually cover your average murder case," Chloe said.

"This isn't your average murder case," Clark said. "It's clearly something more. And you've got the inside scoop, Chloe."

She nodded. "I guess I do."

"Investigative reporters search for good stories, Chloe, and this one just fell in your lap. You've got to run with it, figure out what's going on."

"How do you know so much about investigative journalism, Clark?" she asked. She had never noticed his interest in journalism before, but then, Clark kept many sides of himself hidden.

"I think there's nothing more important than a good journalist, Chloe." He put a hand on her shoulder. "And I think you're one of the best."

CHAPTER TWELVE

The divers finished up at twilight. They scoured the bottom of the marsh, getting covered in weeds and muck. Clark used his X-ray vision as well, and saw nothing else down there, even though he still couldn't get as close to the split oak tree as he wanted to.

One of the cops drove Pete and Lana home around suppertime, but Clark decided to stay with Chloe. He knew she wouldn't leave until the police did—especially not after the speech he'd given her.

He wasn't sure what possessed him to say all of that. It was true he admired her determination, her willingness to go after every important story that came her way. But he also saw what kind of a difference she made around school and sometimes even around Smallville.

He was beginning to realize what kind of an impact a good journalist could make. Chloe had the kind of logical intelligence that made for a good investigator, and she was an excellent writer. She also had a nose for digging out the stories that people wanted hidden.

She was the one who had pushed all of them to come back out here. He wasn't sure he would have done so without her.

At her request, he pocketed her film before Roberts came back to their side of the marsh. That way, when he asked for her film, she could honestly tell him the canister she gave him (of mostly shots of Clark and the marsh) was the only can of film she had.

She would gather the rest from Clark later.

Roberts hurried past them without a word, but Chloe managed to corner one of the divers before he made it back to the cars. The medical examiner was still near the oak, dealing with the bodies. Some of the other officers were helping him.

Davies apparently was scouring the area, looking for clues they'd obviously missed.

The diver walked toward Chloe and Clark, pulling off his mask as he came. His skin was red from the pressure of the mask, and he still had some weeds and algae along his chin.

He seemed a lot younger than Clark expected him to be. It made Clark wonder if the diver was actually a police officer or just someone they'd gotten from around the area, someone who knew how to use a tank and search underwater.

Chloe hurried toward the diver, going ankle deep in muck. "Excuse me," she said. "I don't mean to bother you, but—"

"I'm not supposed to talk to anyone," the diver said. He sounded weary. His voice cracked as he spoke.

"I know," Chloe said. "But we're the ones—"

"You're the ones I was warned against," the diver said. "The detective in charge said you were nosy kids."

Chloe's back straightened, but she didn't bristle like Clark would have expected her to. "We're not nosy," she said. "Clark here is the one who found Danny. He went into the pond up at the top of the property without a mask or diving equipment, and he pulled Danny out."

Clark felt his cheeks heat up. The diver raised his head and looked past Chloe at Clark. The diver's expression was cool, as if he thought what Clark had done was ridiculous.

"You pulled a body out?" the diver asked.

"I thought he might still be alive." Even to his own ears, Clark sounded sheepish.

The diver nodded. "I've done that once or twice. Kind of a shock when the skin's so cold, isn't it?"

"And slimy," Clark said. "That's really what got me."

"Did it move on you? Slide over the bone? That sensation comes to me in dreams sometimes."

Chloe shuddered. She opened her mouth as if she were going to say something, then changed her mind.

Clark extended his hand. "I'm Clark Kent."

The diver took it. "Mike Hawthorne. I'm just a volunteer, you know. Lowell County doesn't have the dollars to keep a diver on staff. They could use a few other folks who've got the experience."

"I've never done diving," Clark said.

"I could train you. Lord knows, I don't want to do this all the time." Hawthorne sounded weary.

"I hear you," Clark said. "I don't think I'll ever get past seeing Danny like that."

"He was a friend of yours?"

"I've known him most of my life," Clark said.

"Harsh." Hawthorne walked past Chloe as if she wasn't even there. She trailed after him. "I can't believe you thought he was alive, though. Not with his skull messed up like that."

"His skull wasn't messed up," Clark said. "He looked pretty normal—except, you know, the bruising and his skin color."

The image of Danny's bluish white skin rose in Clark's mind again, and he had to forcibly make the image disappear.

"Normal? You're kidding, right? I thought the other two bodies were from the same crime as these."

"I don't know," Clark said. "All we could tell was one of them looked like it might be Bonnie from a distance. You know, one of the twin daughters."

Hawthorne nodded. "Her and her mother. Both shot in the head."

"Shot?!" Chloe exclaimed, then put her hands over her mouth.

Hawthorne started as if he'd just remembered she was there. "I shouldn't be talking about this."

"Danny wasn't shot," Clark said. "Neither was his other sister."

Hawthorne glanced behind him, at the oak tree and the medical examiner, still working over the bodies. Clark wondered what the examiner had to do that took so long. Probably photograph their condition and make some kind of preliminary report before getting them back to his lab.

"These two were definitely shot," Hawthorne said. "You can sometimes miss the entry wound, but exit wounds like that . . ."

His voice trailed off, then he shook his head.

Chloe was still looking at the tree. Clark recognized her expression. She wanted to go over and photograph the bodies. She didn't dare. They were in enough trouble already.

"I didn't tell you any of this, by the way," Hawthorne said. "You didn't hear it from me."

"I didn't hear anything," Clark said. "But thanks for talking to us."

"Wish I could say it was my pleasure. You know, when I got my certification, I never figured I'd be doing stuff like this." He trudged off, ducking beneath the opening in the underbrush.

Chloe slogged toward Clark. He finally reached out and helped her onto firmer ground. Her legs were brown below the knees and caked with mud from the ankles on so badly that the only way he knew she was wearing shoes was by the shape of her feet.

"Shot," she said softly. "I can't believe it."

"It caught me by surprise," Clark said.

"Well, that shows there was more than one killer," Chloe said.

"It doesn't show anything, except that the killer was determined." Clark kept his voice down. He didn't want to take the chance of Roberts overhearing them and yelling at Hawthorne for giving out the information.

"I don't see it, Clark. Two different locations, two different methods of killing."

Clark pulled Chloe closer. She was shivering. He had to get her home. "I'm not an expert, Chloe. But it seems to me that one guy could have started out using his hands, kind of unplanned. Then his wife or daughter walks in on him with a gun, he grabs it away, and shoots the remaining members of the family or whatever."

"I thought you thought that Jed Franklin didn't do this."

"I thought you thought that," Clark said.

"I thought you thought the same way I did," Chloe said.

"I usually do," Clark said.

She nodded. "Then you should be confused by this news."

"I am." He sighed. "I have no idea what's going on. I just know that an entire family is gone."

"Except the father."

"Who has been under suspicion from the start."

"Don't you find that odd?" Chloe asked. "I mean, women kill their families, too."

"Only we know now that Mrs. Franklin didn't do it."

"Yeah, we do know that." Chloe looked down. "Man, am I a mess. Not only am I going to be late for dinner, I'm coming home a total wreck again."

"I thought you called your folks."

"And got the machine," Chloe said. "Let's just hope they checked it before Mom set the table."

Clark nodded. He had spoken to his mom, who had urged

him to come home. He had told her, though, that he wanted to stay with Chloe, and his mom agreed that that would be a good idea.

The dappled sunlight had long since disappeared from this section of woods. The light had a whitish cast that Clark knew was a prelude to twilight. It would get dark faster in the marsh than it would anywhere else.

A mosquito buzzed past him, not landing on him as usual. Bugs swarmed around Chloe. She wiped a hand over her face, leaving a trail of mud.

"I hate being a wreck," she said.

Clark smiled at her. "You're fine."

She shook her head and trudged past him, her shoes making sloshing sounds. Mosquitoes trailed her as if she were the best meal they'd seen in weeks. Pete would have been happy to note that she was now getting that treatment.

Clark hurried to keep up with her. She went through the hole in the brambles as if she'd been doing it all her life. He followed, the branches barely tickling him as they had done before.

He was happy to be leaving this place. It had such a feeling of loss and sadness to it. Whoever had chosen to hide the bodies here couldn't have picked a better spot.

The way the bodies were hidden was one of the many things about this case that bothered him. Now he could add the fact that two bodies were shot and two were strangled. Two were placed in one pond, which was easy to see, and two were placed in a marsh no one but the family knew about.

The house had been trashed, the truck was gone, and there was still one family member unaccounted for.

None of it made any sense.

Clark came out of the tangle and nearly ran into Chloe.

She was standing right in front of the opening, Deputy Davies beside her.

". . . didn't realize you were still here," Davies was saying to her.

Clark stood up behind her. Davies looked up at him.

"Both of you," Davies amended.

"We wanted to stay until we knew what was going on," Chloe said.

"Do you now?" Davies asked.

Chloe shook her head. "I can't speak for Clark, but I'm more confused than ever."

"We won't know what's going on until we have all the forensic evidence," Davies said. "We're working off too many theories right now."

"All of them having to do with Jed Franklin?" Clark asked.

Chloe looked at him sideways—her approving look. Apparently that was the question she would have asked.

"Frankly, it wouldn't surprise me if we found his body in the woods nearby—or in his truck not too far from here," Davies said.

"You think someone else murdered him, too?" Chloe asked.

"Self-inflicted gunshot wound, right?" Clark asked.

"You got it," Davies said. "We'll be combing this area all night. We owe a lot to you kids."

"I wish Detective Roberts would realize that," Chloe said. "He's been rude right from the beginning, as if he suspects us."

"You guys check out," Davies said.

Clark felt a shiver of surprise run through him. Chloe frowned at Davies. "You checked us out?"

"Of course we did," Davies said. "Alibis, school history, everything. We'd've been remiss if we hadn't."

"And we checked out," Clark said dryly.

"Checked out on the alibis and on the personality traits." Davies grinned at Chloe. "I believe Principal Kwan said that you were 'persistent' when you felt you had a story, and that your friends were always quite helpful in making sure you got that story."

"Leave it to Principal Kwan," Chloe muttered.

"Hmm?" Davies asked.

Chloe shook her head. "So we're not in trouble with Roberts?"

"I don't think you ever were." Davies looked around as if he were scouting for Roberts.

Several sheriff's cars were parked all over the yard, and deputies, many in uniform, were going into the wooded areas nearby. Clark didn't see Roberts, but that meant nothing. The man had the ability to appear out of nowhere.

"Then I don't understand," Chloe said. "Why's he been so mean?"

Davies looked at her in surprise. "Mean?"

"He hasn't believed us from the beginning. He's accused us of all kinds of things, and he was really angry this afternoon when we found the marsh."

Davies shoved his hands in his pockets. Clark took a step closer to Chloe. For some reason, he felt like he needed to protect her back.

"He's not mean," Davies said after a moment's consideration. "He's frustrated, and probably angry at himself."

"Why?" Clark asked.

"He was the one who got the files after Franklin's arrest last week. He was supposed to follow up. He never did."

Clark could feel Chloe snap to alert. "Franklin was arrested last week? How come that wasn't released?"

"It was." Davies gave her a sideways smile. "In that thing

most reporters ignore, the weekly arrest report. It rarely hits the paper outside of small towns."

"Does the *Torch* get that?" Clark asked.

"No," Chloe said. "If you have someone on the police beat, they get to look at it or make a copy or something. But there's no one on any beat. Just me."

And Clark heard her unspoken thoughts: normally, she thought such things like police beats and city council reports beneath her.

"What was he arrested for?" Chloe asked.

"I don't remember," Davies said. "Disturbing the peace, drunk and disorderly, something."

"That wouldn't require a detective's follow-up, would it?" Clark asked.

Davies shook his head. "I don't know the details. I'd tell you to ask Roberts about it, but the subject's a sensitive one at the moment."

"He's blaming himself for this?" Clark asked.

Davies nodded. "If he'd followed up, maybe none of this would have happened."

"Or maybe he would have died, too," Chloe said with her usual practicality. She put a hand on Clark's arm. "C'mon, Clark. The mud's drying here, and pretty soon, I won't be able to move my legs."

"You want me to drive?" he asked, a little worried at the clip she would take going home, considering the new information.

"I'm fine," she said, and headed to the car.

Clark stopped by Davies. "Thanks for talking to us."

He nodded, looking beyond Clark at the farmhouse. "Figured we owed you guys something," Davies said. "We'd've been wondering about the wife and sister for a long time if you hadn't found the marsh. We'll do a more thorough search this time. I'll see to it."

Clark nodded at him, then went to the passenger seat of the car. As he folded himself in it, he realized that he was covered with mud as well. It flaked off him, landing on the seat and the floorboards.

"Sorry about that," he said to Chloe.

But she stared at it for a long moment, not saying a word. "There hasn't been rain for nearly four days now," she said after a moment.

"So?" Clark asked.

"There was rain last week. Imagine how muddy the marsh was then."

"And how covered with mud the killer got," he said.

She nodded, then started the car and put it into gear. She spun around the gravel turnaround, and headed up the road, the car bouncing the entire way.

"I thought you weren't going to drive fast," Clark said.

"That was before I had two new pieces of information." Chloe grinned at him. "We might be able to crack this case yet."

CHAPTER THIRTEEN

Darkness had fallen across Metropolis, but the city was never dark. It had an ambient light, composed of streetlights, neon, and spots, that made the entire city seem to glow from within.

Lex had forgotten about nights in the city, forgotten how they lured him to leave the building, drink his troubles away, dance with women he'd never seen before, and invent new troubles, just to irritate his father.

His father. Lex turned away from the wall of windows in his father's office. There had been no word from the kidnappers all day, and that worried Lex. As the FBI guys said, the kidnappers weren't following the script—and any deviation from that script did not bode well for Lionel Luthor.

Word had leaked to the news media, of course. The banner headlines around the square just a few blocks away proclaimed in large red letters: KIDNAPPERS SILENT . . . NO WORD ON LOCATION OF FINANCIER LIONEL LUTHOR.

The front page of the *Daily Planet* ran one of the pictures of Lex's father, and asked people to identify the location, if they could. Other newspapers followed suit, and the local all-news channel had been running the digital clip ever since the police leaked it to them.

The police or the FBI. Either way, Lex was not happy about it. He didn't want any word of this case in the press, and now it was the day's main story.

That and the decline of LuthorCorp stock. The stock had plummeted dramatically again, and no amount of speechifying by Lex or the board of directors seemed to make a difference. If this decline continued, there wouldn't be a company for Lionel Luthor to come back to.

If, indeed, he was coming back.

Lex turned away from the windows, surprised to see a diminutive man standing in front of his desk. The man hadn't been reflected in the glass; for one fanciful moment, Lex thought him a vampire.

But the man's reflection showed up in the other wall of windows. He had just been standing behind Lex so that Lex hadn't been able to see him.

Crafty. But not as crafty as Lex could be.

"Who let you in here?" Lex asked.

"The secretary." The man had a Boston Brahmin accent. Lex couldn't tell if it was real or fake. The man's hair had been cut in the Kennedy style, short in front and long around the ears, and he wore a conservative black suit that could have come out of the early sixties.

Even his tie was too long and narrow.

"Well," Lex said, "she made a mistake. No one's supposed to be in this room."

"Not even you, right, Lex?"

Lex made his eyes go flat. It was a look that usually cowed people. It didn't seem to bother this guy. "I don't believe we've been properly introduced."

The man took a step forward, and extended his hand. "Reginald Dewitt. I'm the lead FBI agent assigned to your father's case."

Lex looked down at the offered hand. It was manicured, the nails buffed and groomed. Not your average FBI agent, but then, Lex knew the FBI culture in Metropolis was different than the rest of the country. At the upper echelons, this was considered the dream assignment, and a lot of guys took the perks.

Apparently this guy did.

"Identification?" Lex said.

Dewitt stared at Lex for a moment, then withdrew his hand. He reached into the pocket of his suit coat and removed a golden shield with the FBI logo. Lex took it, studied it, resisted the urge to bite it, the way people did in movies to see if gold was real.

He'd seen a lot of FBI badges in the past. This one was legit. He almost wished it wasn't.

"How come I didn't meet you yesterday?" Lex asked.

"Yesterday, I was in London," Dewitt said.

"Not working on my dad's case." Lex handed him back the badge.

"Believe it or not, there are other things we do."

"Oh, I believe it." Lex walked behind his father's desk, made sure the drawers were closed, and nothing revealing showed on the running computer screen. "I'm just wondering why they didn't keep you at your post and let the original guys handle this."

"I have more experience with high-level matters," Dewitt said. "A lot of people are concerned about your father's case."

"Who called you in?" Lex asked. "Because I know I sure as hell didn't."

"Given your experience with law enforcement, that's not a surprise." Dewitt could make his eyes go flat as well. Impressive, for someone who wore a designer knock-off suit and drew a government paycheck.

"I don't like dancing with someone I just met," Lex said. "Are you going to tell me who brought you in, or am I going to get security to throw you out?"

"You're probably going to call security anyway," Dewitt said.

Lex reached for the phone.

"Let's just say some very important people have investments in LuthorCorp, and after the other stock market debacles these past few years, they're not too keen on having another."

"Sounds like they're panicking," Lex said. "When my father gets back—"

"We both know that the longer these kidnappers remain silent, the less chance there is for your father to get out alive. Our people have been looking at the video and the photographs. We've got a line on the place the fax was sent from, and we hope to know where the e-mail came from shortly. We're going to take care of this, Lex, and get your father one way or another."

"Are you telling me or asking me? Or just blowing smoke?" Lex asked. He kept his voice calm, but he gripped the side of the desk so hard his fingers hurt. He had all the information that the FBI was just beginning to get. They were probably interfering with his investigation, although he didn't want to tell Dewitt that.

"I'm telling you," Dewitt said, "because I believe that part of the problem here could be you."

Lex felt his cheeks heat. He shouldn't have come into his father's office in the first place. He always felt inadequate in here. "Oh?"

"I understand you have been contacted by the kidnappers with a specific sum of money, yet you've done nothing to assemble that money."

"I thought you don't give kidnappers what they want," Lex said.

"Making a pretense is a good idea," Dewitt said. "My techs tell me these guys have some knowledge of computers. They might be able to monitor LuthorCorp accounts, to know if you're assembling funds. You haven't done anything today except go clubbing, talk to the press about LuthorCorp, and hole up in the office."

Lex felt anger, as cold as a midwinter wind, run through him. Clubbing? So they were following him, but apparently they hadn't gone inside Club Noir. Perhaps they thought Lex had kidnapped his own father.

That would explain the discussion now.

And, given Lex's background, it wouldn't be that far-fetched, although it was a bit—Roman emperorish—for his tastes.

"Perhaps I have access to funds you people know nothing about," he said.

"We know a lot," Dewitt said.

"Have you run the fingerprints yet? The ones from the Internet café where the e-mail was sent from?"

Dewitt started. "What are you—?"

"This afternoon, we sent over one of your guys to an Internet café five blocks from where my father was kidnapped. The owner was saving a keyboard for us. The keyboard had been used to send the e-mail. I know your guy brought the keyboard back. I even know that the prints were taken, and sent to the FBI database. What I don't know is if they had a hit."

It was Dewitt's turn to flush. "No one told me—"

"Of course not," Lex said, "because you're committing an end run around someone else's investigation. Has no one told you that this is the worst way to handle a case like this? Because if your subordinates won't, I will. I want you out of here."

Dewitt frowned at him. "I'm here by orders of—"

"I don't care if you're here by orders of God," Lex said. "You can leave. We're handling this on our own."

He punched the intercom on his dad's phone system. "Send security in here. Have them escort Mr. Dewitt out of the building, and make sure he does not gain access again."

"Yes, sir," his father's secretary responded.

"Mr. Luthor, you're going to regret this. I have expertise that no one else—"

"Mr. Luthor?" Lex asked. "A moment ago, it was Lex."

"My mistake," Dewitt said. "You're going to want my help. The financial matters alone will be tricky, and while the team we have downstairs is a good one, they haven't worked as many of these cases as I have."

Lex heard the main doors outside the office open. "Tell me, Mr. Dewitt. Of all the cases you handled, how many of the victims came back alive?"

"Enough," Dewitt said.

"How many?" Lex asked.

"Five," Dewitt said.

"Out of?"

"One hundred."

"So the Big Cheese, whoever that might be, sent me a guy with a 95 percent failure rate? Fascinating. Maybe I should start investigating the FBI and see if they're behind this thing with my father."

"Mr. Luthor—"

The doors to the office opened. Two burly security men that Lex didn't recognize walked in, followed by Hensen, the FBI man who had been in charge up until now. Hensen glared at Dewitt, and Lex noted the hatred in both men's gazes.

"Mr. Luthor," Dewitt said, turning away from Hensen and the guards, "none of the companies was hurt financially in any way, and there were no leaks to the press. To this day, most people do not know what happened. I managed to keep the situation under wraps and to protect the assets involved better than any other man in the field ever had."

Lex let his gaze go flat again. "You think the assets are the most important thing to me?"

"You're not touching them. There has to be a reason for it."

"Perhaps because I've read the FBI playbook as well. I know that giving kidnappers what they want is no better than failing to give them what they want. The best thing to do is quick forensic work, figuring out where the victim is, and sending in a team to rescue him."

"That hasn't worked either, Mr. Luthor. In all such cases, the victims die when a team goes in."

"Then the team screwed up." Lex waved his hand at the guards. "Get him out of here."

"Mr. Luthor, I wasn't brought here by you. The director of the FBI personally made certain that I would be the one in charge. You can't change that." Dewitt held his ground.

Lex smiled at him. Lex made certain the smile was cold. "You're right. I can't change that. But I can make certain you have no access whatsoever to this building, my people, or any information that we obtain first."

"I wouldn't advise you to get involved—"

"And I am making it clear what I think your advice is worth. Gentlemen, I'm not telling you again. Get him out of this building, or I'll find someone who will."

The guards grabbed Dewitt, who shook them off. He headed for the door, still glaring at Hensen. Then he looked at Lex. "You'll—"

"Regret this?" Lex shrugged one shoulder. "I doubt it. A man who can't be more creative on his parting shot is not worth my time, and is certainly not someone who should be in charge of this case."

The guards pushed Dewitt out of the room. Hensen started to follow.

"Mr. Hensen," Lex said. "Any progress?"

"You know where we stand, sir." Hensen pushed the door closed.

"I got you those fingerprints this afternoon," Lex said.

"Yes, sir. We've sent them to the database, but there's a queue—"

"Jump the queue," Lex said. "If the director of the FBI is personally worried about LuthorCorp, then he should be able to authorize a rush order on those prints."

"Yes, sir, although they're not going to be happy that the request comes from me. Not after this." Hensen looked over his shoulder at the closed door.

"It doesn't come from you, Agent Hensen." Lex spoke softer than he had before. He always spoke softly when he was angry. "It comes from me. I'll speak to your boss directly if I have to."

"I'm sure that won't be necessary, sir."

"Good." Lex sat down at his father's desk. The chair was uncomfortable—built for his father, and not for Lex.

Hensen waited.

"That's all," Lex said.

Hensen left, pulling the door closed behind him. Lex put his hand over his face and closed his eyes. It was all a bluff to him. He had no real idea what he was doing. All he knew was that he didn't want to get caught in some government agency's power plays. Besides, Dewitt wouldn't have allowed Lex to run things his way. Hensen was easy to manipulate.

The computer screen before him flickered to life. He'd had his e-mail routed in here, and now an envelope blinked on the screen. He opened it.

It was from Brodsky, although it didn't say that. There was no address in the From category, and the subject line read "Noir."

There was no message, just four jpeg files. The first was a black-and-white photograph of three men, loitering near City Bank. The men held hats in their hands, and two of the men had spray canisters. They all had thick beards that partially obscured their faces. The third man looked familiar—and not because he was the guy at the Internet café.

Lex had the feeling he'd seen that man before.

The men were white, burly, and overdressed for the heat of that day. The third man was looking toward the street, a frown on his face.

Lex wondered what Brodsky thought was so important about the photograph—besides the fact that Brodsky believed the men to be the perpetrators of the kidnapping. If Brodsky had this photo, he had others as well. They were frames from the bank's security video. There was some other bit of information in the frame that Lex should see, but didn't.

He closed that file, vowing to come back to it, and opened the next. It, too, was from the security video. It showed a red truck, brand-new, with Kansas plates, parked in the handicapped parking spot in front of one of the buildings across the street. The license number was obscured, but Lex got part of it.

He would be able to use that.

Then he went to the third photograph. It was a section of the curtain that had been behind his father in the still photograph. A hand hung there, as if it had gotten caught in the picture by accident.

The hand was reddish and dark brown. A spring sunburn over skin that normally tanned. On the ring finger, a plain gold wedding band, scratched and worn with time.

Again, information that Brodsky saw that Lex didn't. He'd have to think about it. Or maybe the fourth photograph would put it all into perspective.

He opened the last file. The photograph came from the digital video of his unconscious father. His father's ear and the top of his skull were fuzzed in the front of the frame. In the back, in focus, was a window. Outside the window, trees. Just trees.

So they had him in the country.

Lex looked again at the other photographs. Kansas plates, men who didn't belong, and that sunburned hand. Someone who worked outdoors. Maybe it was his property. If Lex found out the license number of the truck, he would find the men.

He glanced at the first photograph again. That was it. Not just the faces, but the boots. No one wore work boots in Metropolis. Only out-of-towners and young men trying to make a political statement. These men weren't young, and they weren't making that kind of statement.

They were after something else.

A knock sounded on his door. Lex sighed and hit the intercom. "I don't want to be disturbed," he said.

There was a moment of silence. He realized that the secretary was away from her desk. He sighed. He had the urge to fire her, but he kept thinking of his father, wondering if he wanted the eye candy gone.

His father, who might never come back.

Then the intercom beeped. "Sir, it's Hensen. We have a match on the print."

"Bring it in, then," Lex said.

The doors opened, and Hensen came in. His suit didn't pretend to belong to a high-end label. It was off-the-rack, ill fitting and brown, certainly not something that belonged in Metropolis.

He was carrying a sheet of paper.

"His name is Thomas Porter," Hensen said. "He did time for a number of things. His record extends back to some sealed juvenile counts. But as an adult, he started with robbery, then armed robbery, and then he moved into high-tech crimes, which put him on a watch list of ours. We had no idea he was in Kansas. Last we heard of him, two years ago, he was in Florida."

"Is this a mug shot?" Lex asked, extending his hand.

"Several," Hensen said, handing him the paper.

Lex brought the paper up and studied it for a moment. Five different mug shots, all from various parts of the country and from various years. The one at the top, the most recent, also showed Porter with a goatee. The man looked somewhat like one of the three standing outside the bank.

Then Lex's gaze fell on the bottom shot, the first mug shot, taken when Porter didn't have any facial hair at all. He gazed directly into the camera, and it almost felt like he was in the room.

Lex had seen that gaze before. He'd actually felt it in person. The anger he'd been feeling since Dewitt invaded the office—actually since Lex's father disappeared—rose up again.

"This man's name may be Thomas Porter," Lex said quietly. "But he worked in the Smallville plant under the name J. B. Bynes. My father ordered me to fire him three months ago."

"Why?" Hensen asked.

Lex set the paper carefully on his father's desk. "Bynes was an agitator. I had other plans for keeping him quiet, but my father believed that agitators should be thrown out quickly. It was the first volley in what would become a serious round of layoffs."

"The layoffs you and your father quarreled about."

Lex looked at Hensen. The man seemed nervous.

"Does everyone in the FBI suspect I'm behind my father's kidnapping?" Lex asked.

Hensen took a deep, nervous breath. "I don't think so, sir."

"But that's why they brought in Dewitt."

"Yes, sir."

One point for Hensen. At least he didn't lie. Lex reached over to the computer, turned on the printer, and printed up the photograph of the three men and the photograph of the truck.

He handed them to Hensen.

"Bynes is clearly involved," Lex said. "Let's find him. I suspect this is his truck. Let's track it down, too. He was in Metropolis as recently as this morning. And if he's the man I remember, he's not the trusting type. He'd have my father nearby so that he can check on him and his guards."

"In the city?" Hensen asked.

"Too suspicious. Too many witnesses." Lex wasn't about to tell Hensen that he knew his father was being kept in the country. "Let's check the countryside first. Use a copter, see if you can see that truck from the air. And start in the areas between Smallville and Metropolis."

"You think he's been planning this for a long time?"

"I don't think it, Hensen," Lex said. "I know it. He wouldn't have come to Smallville in the first place if he weren't. So all of his plans would have focused in that area. We're going to focus there, too."

Hensen nodded. He took the photographs and left the office without waiting to be dismissed.

Lex leaned back in the chair. His stomach twisted. He knew this man, had actually defended him and his job, and had thought of offering him a position that would have used his raw strength and oddly magnetic personality.

Maybe if he had been allowed to do that, none of this would have happened.

Maybe.

But there was no use looking backward. They had a name, they had a face, and they might even have more than one motive.

Now all they had to do was find J. B. Bynes and his hideout.

There was a lot of countryside between Metropolis and Smallville—not all of it cultivated farmland. Bynes was smart. The hideout would be difficult to find.

But that wasn't what worried Lex the most. What worried him the most was Bynes's—or Porter's—rap sheet. The man's criminal activities had escalated his whole life. It wasn't a large step from armed robbery to murder.

And Lex had a hunch that was precisely the direction J. B. Bynes had decided to go.

CHAPTER FOURTEEN

The lights in the *Torch* office were low. Chloe took a handful of M&M's from the bag that sat beside her computer. She ate the candies one at a time, savoring the chocolate.

She had closed the blinds so that no one could see in. Clark would probably yell at her for being here, but she felt time pressure on this case.

Time pressure mixed with guilt. She had a lot more in common with Roberts than she wanted to admit. If she had listened to Danny, then maybe none of this would have happened.

Chloe and Roberts, missing signals. She wondered how many missed signals happened in cases like this where entire families died—how many friends and people in authority looked back and wondered what they could have done differently to prevent it all.

Her hand was shaking slightly. She'd had too much caffeine already, and the night had just begun. Going two days without sleep wouldn't be the brightest thing she ever did, but if it resolved this case, she'd feel vindicated.

She had gone home, taken a shower, eaten the warmed-up dinner that her mother had left for her, then sneaked back out to the *Torch* office. Her parents thought she was in her room asleep, but she had more important things to do. If they needed her, they would know where to find her.

They hated the way she worked so hard on what they considered to be a school project, but at least she wasn't getting into trouble. Or typical trouble anyway—boys, drinking, petty crime.

Even though she wouldn't mind getting into trouble with

boys—one boy in particular. If only Clark would take his gaze off Lana long enough to realize that he and Chloe had a lot more in common.

He had startled her when he had shown that he knew so much about investigative reporting—and when it became clear how much he admired people who did it well. Her cheeks still burned when she thought about that.

She sipped the double tall she'd gotten on the drive over. The coffee was cold now, but still useful. She'd been digging through arrest records, Internet files, and old news reports, looking for information on Jed Franklin.

What she'd found had been unexpected. In his youth, Jed Franklin had gotten arrested a number of times for protesting things like proposed nuclear waste sites here in Kansas, and actions of LuthorCorp outside of Smallville, long before the corporation bought the creamed corn factory from Pete's parents.

Then Jed Franklin's father died, and Jed inherited the farm. He dropped out of college and took over the Franklin property, shutting off parts of it that had always drained resources —like the marsh—and made the farm a viable enterprise. He got married, had a family, and except for the marriage and birth announcements, dropped out of the news.

Until three months ago. Three months ago, he had been laid off from LuthorCorp. He felt that he and a group of others had been dismissed because they were talking to some union representatives about improving working conditions at the plant.

He accused Lex Luthor of lying to him. Lex, according to Franklin, had seemed amenable to talking about making changes that would benefit the workers. Lex didn't want to unionize the plant, but he would do what he could to keep the workers happy.

Franklin had left the meeting feeling optimistic. Two days

later, however, he got word that he and the others who had attended that meeting—in fact everyone whose name had been mentioned in connection with possible union activity—had been laid off.

The layoff notices had come from LuthorCorp offices in Metropolis. The story made the papers—including the *Torch*—and Chloe remembered talking to Lex about it herself.

He had promised to do right by those employees, saying darkly that it was against the law to fire someone for starting union activity. But the next time Chloe contacted him about the layoffs, Lex had said that the decision had nothing to do with unions, and gave her a number in Metropolis to call.

"Just put in your paper that this wasn't my decision," he had said. "My father and I have very different ways of doing things. Unfortunately, I have to follow my father's methods right now."

She had written that, and everyone had said it rang false. But it hadn't sounded false when Lex mentioned it.

Jed Franklin had stopped giving interviews, too. But he spent a lot of time getting drunk in neighborhood bars, talking about how easy it was for money just to disappear. First his farm, then the job he got to save his farm. Now he had no idea what he would do to take care of his family.

No idea at all.

Those words had been part of a puff piece the *Daily Planet* had done on area layoffs—not just at LuthorCorp, but all over the state as the economy went sour. Most people didn't sound as bitter as Franklin; they seemed to have the attitude that they'd get another job.

But Franklin claimed that LuthorCorp was making it impossible for him to get another job, telling anyone he interviewed with that he was a troublemaker and they might think twice about hiring him.

Chloe sipped from her double tall again, only to find the giveaway all-you-can-drink cup from the Talon was empty. She would either have to make herself instant coffee using the tiny microwave she had bought for the *Torch* office, or she'd have to switch to Mountain Dew.

Somehow Mountain Dew didn't seem all that professional to her. But instant coffee didn't sound appealing.

She left her desk, found some old tea bags and a ceramic mug, and microwaved herself some tea. She carried the steaming mug back to her desk and read the last of the files she had found.

Two weeks ago, Franklin assaulted a shift supervisor from the Smallville plant in one of the local bars. The police were called, but the supervisor declined to press charges. Later in the week, Franklin got charged on two different occasions with being drunk and disorderly.

Up until then, he'd been known as one of Smallville's most upstanding citizens. This had to be when the police chief assigned Roberts the Franklin case, maybe just to quiet Franklin down or maybe because the chief believed there was some merit to Franklin's accusations, that LutherCorp was trying to blacklist him.

Chloe found nothing else in the public files. But about ten days ago coincided with the conversation she'd had with Danny. She'd made some notes after they had spoken, force of habit mostly, but sometimes those notes got her future stories.

She took a few more M&M's and found that week's notebook. She thumbed through the pages until she found the page with Danny's comment.

DF says no one understands what's going on there. Thinks his dad has lost it, but not just because of the plant.

Because of two of the guys he's been involved with. Danny doesn't like them, says they're the ones who led his dad down this wrong road. Danny thinks they provoked the Luthors just to start a fight, and that this was about something bigger, but he won't say what.

Chloe turned the pages in her notebook, but found nothing else. No other references, no more notes. Nothing about that desperate look in Danny's eye when he spoke to her.

When she had brushed him off because layoffs simply weren't news.

She hadn't been listening to him, even though she'd recorded his comments. She had assumed he'd been talking about the layoffs, but it sounded like something else, something different.

She went through the news stories, but Franklin's name was the only one that appeared in connection with the layoffs. No one else's.

She needed to find out who else was laid off, what people Danny might have been talking about. Lex was in Metropolis dealing with his father's kidnapping, so Chloe couldn't contact him. But there might be other people at the plant who would be willing to talk. Maybe even that supervisor who refused to press charges. Clearly he had some sympathy for the things Franklin was going through.

All Chloe had to do was find out who he was.

Clark sat in his favorite chair in the loft, his feet on the windowsill. He balanced the chair on its two back legs, staring out at the night sky.

He didn't feel like looking through the telescope tonight. Reflecting on his real parents, where they had come from and what they must have been thinking when they put him into that spaceship didn't seem like idle speculation anymore.

He was looking at the dark side of parenthood now, where people weren't saints, and things could go horribly wrong. He'd always known that, he supposed, but it never hit home to him, at least not until earlier in the year, when his father—a man whose integrity Clark admired beyond all else—had pointed a gun at him.

Granted, his dad hadn't been in his right mind at the time. He'd been under the influence of the Nicodemus plant. But even then, when his father realized who he'd been aiming at, he had stopped—even under the influence.

There was nothing good about the Franklin case. The weight of the additional two bodies felt like something from a dream. The fact that they'd been killed differently seemed worse, somehow. It made the killings seem less random to Clark, even more deliberate. And he couldn't put his finger on why.

"Hey," his father's voice came from the loft stairs. "Mind if I come in?"

Clark turned. His father was carrying a tray with one hand. On it were two soda fountain glasses his mom had gotten at a garage sale.

"Remember when we used to sit up here, look at the stars, and pig out on your mom's famous root beer floats?" his father asked.

Clark brought his chair down on all four legs. "Is that what you have?"

"Two special floats, the right amount of root beer, the perfect amount of ice cream, and, as a special treat, homemade whipped cream."

"Wow, she went all out." Clark grinned at his father. "I guess that means you can come in. But be careful. I'm going to expect this all the time."

His dad chuckled and sat in the other chair. He handed Clark one of the root beer floats and kept one for himself. Then he set the tray on the floor.

The float had a sugary root beer scent. A long-handled ice tea spoon stuck out of the glass along with a straw that bent. His mom had gone all out.

"She's worried about me, huh?" Clark asked.

His dad, taking a bite of ice cream mixed with whipped cream, shook his head. "I think she's feeling lucky and guilty."

"What?"

"Lucky that we have you. Guilty because we have you."

"You're still not making sense, Dad."

His father nodded. "The Franklin thing. I think it has shaken every parent in Smallville. We're all counting our blessings and realizing how close to the edge things can be at times."

His dad didn't remember the gun incident, and Clark had never told him. Clark had never told anyone. So he knew that his dad wasn't thinking of that.

"You're still thinking that Mr. Franklin did it?"

His dad shrugged. "I don't know what to think anymore, Clark. The whole case doesn't make sense."

"Dad," Clark said, taking a spoonful of ice cream. "Don't tell me what you told Mom."

His dad smiled sideways, but kept looking at the stars. "I think he did it, Clark. I think it happened just like you told Chloe. He got caught halfway through and used more extreme measures."

"It still doesn't explain why he hid the bodies," Clark said. "Chloe's been looking this stuff up on-line, and most of these folks don't move the bodies at all."

"I don't think you can say there's any typical killing, Clark. Everyone's different, and everyone snaps differently." His dad's spoon clanked against the glass. "I think this case does show how callous Smallville has become."

"What do you mean?" Clark took a sip of root beer. The float tasted as good as always, but lacked something. Maybe the sense of festive occasion that usually accompanied this treat. He didn't like it being associated with sadness. Still, he drank it anyway, knowing his mother would be disappointed if he didn't.

"I mean since the meteor, and the strange things that have happened because of it, and since the Luthors have come back to town—"

Clark frowned.

"—I know you like Lex, Clark, but he's part of that family, and they seem to set the tone for the town. We're a lot more insular than we used to be. We used to do things for each other, not gossip about each other. I can't help thinking that maybe we should have done more for the Franklins. Maybe if we'd been more of a community, this wouldn't have happened."

"Just yesterday, Dad, you were saying that nothing can be done when people snap."

His dad nodded, then set his float aside half-finished. "I've been rethinking that. It bothered me when I said it. I'm not sure if we could have made a difference with Jed Franklin, but maybe his family wouldn't have felt like they were alone with their problems. Maybe we could have helped his wife and kids find a way out."

"You don't think they were taken by surprise?"

"I don't know," his dad said.

"The police at the farm said that Mr. Franklin had gotten in trouble with the law in the past two weeks. Did you know that?"

"I knew that Jed Franklin was spouting crazy stuff since he got laid off, something about plots to destroy

LuthorCorp, drunken speeches mostly. No one paid a lot of attention."

The root beer stuck in Clark's throat. He made himself swallow. "Plots to take down LuthorCorp?"

His dad nodded. "I overheard one of the rants when I went to the feed and seed store about ten days ago. It was crazy stuff, Clark."

"Don't you think it odd though that Lex's dad got kidnapped at the same time as all of this has been happening?"

His dad looked at Clark. "I hadn't considered it."

"Losing Lionel Luthor would hurt LuthorCorp, right?" Clark asked.

"It already is," his dad said. "Stock prices are going down. There's talk of some kind of audit. The board of directors is getting nervous, especially with the idea that Lex'll inherit his father's voting shares. It's all over the business pages, and it's not pretty."

Clark nodded. "What if this has nothing to do with Jed Franklin? What if this is about LuthorCorp?"

His dad sighed. "Why would the family be killed and not Franklin? If he knew something about a plot, then why not take him out?"

"Maybe they did," Clark said. "It took a while to find the family's bodies. Maybe they just haven't found his yet."

His dad stood and rested a strong hand on Clark's shoulder. "I admire your way of thinking, son. But usually the least complex answer is the correct one."

"How is this plot any less complex than a man killing his entire family?" Clark asked.

"One, unfortunately, is pretty common. I think every state in the nation has been touched by it in the last ten years," his father said. "But taking out a family because one member knew something—that sort of thing went out with the gangsters of the 1930s."

Clark had no response to that. Maybe his father was right. Maybe Clark preferred to think of a conspiracy instead of a single man destroying everything he loved.

But the idea was one they hadn't looked at. One that he and Chloe might be able to investigate tomorrow.

Lionel Luthor wasn't sure if beer was his friend or his enemy. His captors had had a lot of it, and were pretty drunk. No one seemed to notice that he had worked his bonds loose again.

The effort had been a difficult one with the extreme pain in his elbow. Sweat had beaded on his face. If the men hadn't been drinking, they might have noticed that and found it suspicious.

Instead, they were sitting at three different points in the room, arguing about what to do with him.

The leader—the big man with the beard—wanted to kill him. Luthor had sensed that from the beginning. For the leader, Luthor's death seemed almost seductive.

Luthor's original captor was arguing against it, saying the money was worth more to them than some obscure financial disaster. And the third guy, the one who had come in with the leader, was silently listening, drinking beer after beer until his eyes got glassy.

He was the first to pass out.

The other two didn't even notice, as involved as they were in their argument. Luthor noted, though, that even though they were drunk and in the middle of a heated debate, they managed not to use each other's names.

He wished they'd pass out like their friend. When that happened, he knew what he would do.

The truck keys sat on the filthy kitchen counter, next to

one of the John Deere caps. He would sneak across the room, grab the keys, and hurry outside, making no noise at all. Then he would start the truck and drive out of here as fast as he could, doing his best to make sure they didn't follow him.

A cell phone or a gun hidden in the truck would be too much to hope for, of course. From the moment he got free of the ropes until he arrived in the nearest town, he would be on his own.

He knew he'd have to be careful. One mistake, and he would lose what might be his only opportunity.

But he'd never been a man who waited for anyone else to take care of him. If he had done that—if he had had that attitude—he would never have put together LuthorCorp, never have succeeded in business, never have achieved half the things he achieved.

A beer can toppled to the floor and rolled away from the couch. His initial captor had passed out, and apparently the can had slipped through his fingers.

The leader stared at the rolling can as if it were a grenade. He picked up the pistol he had laid on the table and pointed it at the can, tracking it across the floor.

Luthor watched, hoping that the leader wouldn't shoot the can. The man was too drunk to be thinking clearly. A can like that would explode and send shrapnel all over the room.

"Bang," the leader whispered, and then laughed. "Scare you, Mr. Luthor?"

Luthor didn't answer. He wasn't going to bait this man.

The beer can settled in the middle of the floor, rocking back and forth, the remaining liquid sloshing inside. The can had left a trail of foam that extended all the way to the couch.

"Don't want to admit how scared you are, huh?" The leader stood, swayed, and caught himself on the arm of the chair. "Think I'm wrong? Are you worth more alive than you are dead? Time to find out, huh? See if that kid of yours has been gathering my money yet."

"You're monitoring the accounts of my corporation?" Luthor asked.

"What do you think?" The leader walked across the floor to the tiny kitchen. His steps were steadier now.

Luthor hadn't been keeping track of how much the man had actually had to drink. Maybe he wasn't as drunk as Luthor initially thought.

"Because if you are," Luthor said, "and you're using that information to judge Lex, then you're making a mistake."

"I'll bet you think I'm making a bundle of mistakes, Mr. Luthor."

The leader opened the refrigerator and used the door to brace himself as he looked inside.

"Idiots never buy enough beer," he mumbled.

Luthor glanced at the other two. The initial captor was on the couch, in the same position Luthor had first seen him. The snoring was just beginning—little muffled grunts. Pretty soon, Luthor knew from experience, they would become full-blown roars.

The gun lay on the arm of the chair where the leader had been sitting. Careless. Deliberately careless to see what Luthor would do? Or drunk careless?

Luthor wasn't sure yet. But he would find out.

The leader closed the refrigerator door. He was holding another beer can. It took him a moment to get a grip on the pull tab. When he finally got the beer open, the can sloshed, spilling liquid all over the floor.

The entire cabin smelled of beer now, a scent Luthor couldn't abide.

"So," the leader said. "Tell me about my 'mistake.'"

"It's just that Lex has no access to those accounts. He

needs cooperation from the full board or help from my CFO, who happens to be in Canada. Lex's hands are tied."

It was a lie. Luthor didn't have a chief financial officer. He didn't believe in having someone else run his money. The board was easily accessible, but the average person didn't—couldn't—know that.

"CFO?" the leader said. "I expect you expect me to ask you what that is."

Luthor remained quiet.

"I didn't think you had no CFO, Mr. Luthor. Thought you believed too many hands in the money stole the money."

That was one of his pet phrases. This man knew more about him than he had realized.

"LuthorCorp has a CFO," he said. "I don't know where you heard that we didn't."

"The write-ups in *Business Week* and *Fortune*, not to mention those profiles they do in the business section of the *Daily Planet*. They shoulda called yours Portrait of a Control Freak."

The man was probably right. Luthor actually found a bit of humor in the moment. "Then you understand the dilemma. Lex has no access to any real money. If you know my family's history, you know that my son isn't exactly—reliable."

"Hell." The leader grabbed a wooden-backed chair, and sat in it backwards, bracing the beer on his knee. "If I had a choice between trusting you or trusting him, I'd pick him any day."

"Would you?" Luthor was finding this conversation fascinating. Where had this man gained his opinions of Lex and LuthorCorp? He sounded almost as if he had personal experience.

"Sure. Lex seems to understand the working man. You never have."

Luthor shook his head. "You people fail to realize that I am a working man. I built my fortune from the ground up. I was once a man with no means, and I made myself into someone. People like you seem to think the world owes you money, owes you wealth. You don't want to work for it."

"'People like me?'" the leader said softly. "What do you know about me, Mr. Lionel Luthor?"

"Only that you believe breaking the law is the best way to make a dollar. And that you're probably a control freak, just like you accuse me of being. Except that you like having people in your control. People who are more powerful than you are."

The leader was across the floor in half an instant. He grabbed Luthor by the hair and pulled his head back, straining Luthor's neck. The man bumped Luthor's injured arm as he did so, and ripples of pain ran through Luthor's body.

"I got complete control over you, Luthor. Don't you forget it."

The man smelled of beer. His eyes were red-rimmed and his cheeks were flushed.

Luthor didn't say anything. After a moment, the man released him, shoving him forward. The chair tilted dangerously for a moment, then righted itself.

"You'll never have complete control over me," Luthor said. "You can beat me, hurt me, or kill me, but you'll never break me, and you'll never control me."

The man's eyes narrowed. "Don't give me a challenge like that."

"I feel rather safe in doing so," Luthor said. "You don't have the patience to defeat me."

The man slapped him across the mouth so hard that Luthor bit his tongue.

"'Violent delights,'" Luthor said, tasting blood as he quoted Shakespeare, "'have violent ends.'"

The man yanked him backwards, pulling him so close that their faces almost touched. Luthor's arm was pinched between the chair and the man's leg. The pain was exquisite.

"You ever wondered, Luthor, what happens to everything a man learns when he dies?"

Luthor stared up at those eyes, realizing that they weren't the eyes of a drunk at all.

"I think," the man said, "the knowledge just goes away. Poof! Vanished. Gone. Nothing left. It's why I never bothered to learn nothing that I couldn't use later—not to batter someone with words, but to actually put to use."

"Yes," Luthor said, his voice strangled by the position of his head. "I see how well this plan has worked for you."

The man shoved the chair away again, and this time it fell on its side. Luthor landed on the arm again, and the pain was so intense that his entire world turned white for a brief moment.

He blinked, then opened his eyes. The trail of beer ran past him like a tiny river. The man was crouched in front of him. When he saw that Luthor was awake, he kicked him as hard as he could in the kidneys.

Luthor's breath left his body.

The man grinned. "If I decide to kill you here and now, there's no one to stop me, Luthor. Those idiots are passed out. It's just you and me."

Luthor stared up at him, trying to not gasp for air.

"What I like best about it," the man said, "is that I can take my time. Rather like you do when you decide to destroy someone. I can do it one punch—"

And with that he brought his fist down on Luthor's neck, making Luthor choke.

"—and one kick at a time."

The boot found his ribs again. Luthor closed his eyes. He

wouldn't give this monster the satisfaction of seeing pain, however involuntary.

Luthor braced himself for a long night of violence—and hoped that somehow he would survive.

CHAPTER FIFTEEN

Clark deliberately missed the school bus the next morning. He waited until the bus was around the corner before he used his superspeed to head into Smallville. Running that fast, faster than anyone could see him move, always gave him a thrill. While he was moving that fast his super-vision seemed to slow the world down around him, letting him place his feet perfectly, never missing a step. It was as if the entire world slowed down instead of him speeding up.

He stopped at the Talon, bought Chloe the House Caffeine Special, made with chocolate and a triple shot of espresso, and then hurried, again using his speed to get him past any distractions, and to school.

He knew where he would find her—and he was right.

She was asleep in front of her computer in the *Torch* office, the lights on low the way she had had them all night, and the blinds drawn.

Clark opened the blinds first, letting in the morning sunshine. Chloe groaned. He set down the coffee beside her, along with the pastry he'd picked up at the same time, then stood back.

"This is not fair," Chloe said. She wiped her hair out of her face. "Whoever invented morning should have been stopped."

"I hope you brought your own clothes last night," Clark said, "because I don't think Lana has anything else that she can loan you."

Chloe groped for the coffee, pulled off the lid, and took a sip. "Oh, Clark. You got me real caffeine."

"I got you a buzz that'll last until next week." He sat down. "I hope your work last night turned up something."

"It did." She took a bite of the pastry. "This is good too. You're a saint, Clark."

He felt his cheeks flush. "Don't get carried away."

"Don't mind me," she said. "I'm delirious from lack of sleep."

She took another bite of the pastry. Clark was glad he had done this for her. He couldn't remember seeing her look so wan—at least not when she was healthy. It was more than lack of sleep. This case had gotten to her, just as it had gotten to him and his parents.

"Well?" he asked. "What did you learn?"

She chased the last bit of pastry down with some coffee, swallowed, and said, "I'm not sure what to make of this, but I have a hunch that somehow everything is tied to LuthorCorp."

Clark frowned. "I'm beginning to think everything in Smallville is tied to LuthorCorp."

"Well, it does seem that way." Chloe seemed to be gaining animation as the caffeine and sugar hit. "But I found some strange things."

She told Clark about her findings—Jed Franklin's arrest record, the fact that he once had made the farm a going concern, but somehow lost control of it, the work he did at LuthorCorp, and his strangeness the last few weeks, including his arrests.

Then she took a deep breath and drank some more coffee. Clark could tell she wasn't quite done with her story, so he gave her time to gather herself.

"Clark," Chloe said. "Danny Franklin asked me to write a story on the layoffs. He said they weren't what they seemed, that there was something funny going on. I blew him off . . ."

Her voice trailed away, and she looked down, but not before Clark saw her eyes fill with tears. So that was why she was fighting this story so hard. She felt guilty, too, just like Roberts did. Just like Lana did.

Had the entire community failed these people? Maybe Clark's dad was right. It certainly did seem that way.

"Anyway," Chloe said after a moment. "I'm wondering if we shouldn't check this out. There might be something to it."

Clark nodded. "Last night my dad told me he'd heard one of Jed Franklin's rants. I guess Mr. Franklin was talking about some kind of plot to take down LuthorCorp."

"Do you think he knew about the kidnapping?" Chloe asked.

"That's what I said to my dad, but my dad dismissed it. Said Mr. Franklin was spouting 'crazy stuff.' But I don't know. Maybe he wasn't."

"That still doesn't explain what happened to the family."

"Maybe someone came to kill Franklin and ended up getting everyone," Clark said.

"And they just haven't found Franklin's body yet."

"Exactly."

Chloe stood up. She seemed to be her old self again, energetic and interested. "We've got to track down this plot, Clark."

"We've got American Lit in half an hour, Chloe. I think the investigation can wait until after school."

"Can it?" Chloe asked. "What if we track down the kidnappers?"

"Now you're dreaming," Clark said. "At best, all we're going to figure out is what was going through Jed Franklin's mind in the past week. And I'm not even sure we're going to get that."

"I fell asleep figuring I needed to talk to some of the others who were laid off at the plant," Chloe said. "How about you go to American Lit and take notes, and I go to LuthorCorp to get names?"

"How about we both go to American Lit, and then we talk to this guy I know during lunch," Clark said. "He'll probably be able to tell us the names of everyone laid off from LuthorCorp since the plant opened here."

Chloe shook her head. "Why're you pushing class, Clark?"

"Because, Chloe. The *Torch* isn't the *Washington Post*, and you're not Woodward or Bernstein. You're not going to bring down a president today."

"But I might solve a murder and a kidnapping," she said, grinning at him.

"And then what?" Clark asked. "Most newspapers hire people who've graduated from journalism school, Chloe, and to get into the best journalism schools, you need good grades. You can't skip class whenever you're on the trail of something hot."

She grabbed her book bag. "If I didn't like you so much, Clark Kent, I'd be really annoyed at the fact that you're right all the time."

"So you're coming to class?"

"If you take me to this source of yours."

"I promise." She shook the book bag at him. "And yes, I did bring my own clothes this time. So I'll see you in class."

"I'm expecting you there, Chloe."

"Yes, sir, Truant Officer Kent. I'll be right there, sir." And, still smiling, she flounced out of the room.

Clark sat there for another minute. On days like this, he didn't like the restrictions of going to school any more than Chloe did. But he knew how his parents would feel if he cut class to follow a hunch.

Besides, he and Chloe were trying to solve murders, not save someone from dying. He had a hunch his parents wouldn't mind if he missed class to save someone's life. But to solve a case, that was entirely different.

Even though it didn't feel that way.

Lex had gotten a few fitful hours of sleep on the couch in his office. He had vacated his father's office somewhere around midnight when he had the thought that working in there made him feel like his father wasn't going to come back.

Sunlight pouring into the wall of windows had woken him out of a dream in which his father was a Roman emperor, dying at the hands of his subjects, while Lex stood on a nearby hill and played the fiddle.

He didn't like it that his brain was casting him as the careless Nero. The message was one he didn't want to contemplate.

Lex had also sent an order to personnel to get him a real secretary, not someone who looked like she should grace the pages of *Playboy*. His father's secretary was still on the job—he had sent her home, though, at ten, making her promise to return at her usual time—but he really wanted a competent person who knew how to create office miracles.

The first miracle his new secretary had to perform was to get Lex a nourishing breakfast and more coffee than any human could drink. He wanted everything piping hot, and he also insisted on tasty.

Mrs. Anderson—reassuringly middle-aged and gray-haired—had managed that task with aplomb. He was eating eggs Benedict, and eyeing the stack of pastries that sat on his desk. The coffee, hot, fresh, and tasty, was the best he'd ever tasted in Metropolis.

He was looking at satellite photographs that Hensen had

gotten from some government agency. They were photos of the areas between Metropolis and Smallville, taken just after dawn.

There were even more remote rural areas than he had thought. His impression of Kansas, the state he'd always called his home, was of flat prairies and rolling farmland. He had forgotten just how many wooded areas there were, and how many secluded rivers and streams ran throughout those places.

Kansas, though, had a bloody history of outlaws and fugitives. The James Gang had gotten its start here, not to mention the actual war fought on the land in the years before the Civil War started. They called the state Bloody Kansas then. The marauders had found a whole bunch of places to hide, and had never been caught.

Lex shook off the thoughts. They would catch the people who held his father, and they would get his father back. Alive.

Not that his father would reward him for that.

Part of Lex's complex emotional reaction to this entire ordeal was a concern—as time went on—that he would pull his father from near-certain death and his father, instead of complimenting him, would say, *Leave it to you, Lex, to take so long.*

Suddenly, the eggs Benedict didn't taste good any longer. Lex grabbed his coffee mug and stood. He went to his computer and saw that another e-mail was blinking for him.

He'd set Brodsky another task last night. He wanted Brodsky and his team of hackers to find out everything they could about Porter a.k.a. J. B. Bynes.

Lex clicked open the e-mail program. Sure enough, the e-mail waiting for him, amidst the e-lists he was on, the various business letters he got, and a whole slew of requests for e-interviews from reporters, was a note from Brodsky.

The e-mail note was short and to the point.

```
Our boy rents an apartment in Smallville,
as I'm sure you know. The address is
probably in your corporate database.
However, he has no real reason to rent
since he owns some property in the next
county. County records show a building on
that site, but do not register an owner. In
fact, records indicate that the owner is
absentee, living in California. Some
research led me to the fact that the owner,
listed as one B.J. Ropter is actually our
friend Porter/Bynes.

Address listed below. Area map at this URL.

Have Fun . . .
```

Lex clicked on the URL. His Internet program opened quickly and he found himself staring at a piece of property large enough to hide several houses in. The property was off a county road. Survey work had been done for another road leading onto the property, but, according to the map, the road hadn't yet been built.

Lex checked the map's date. It was a year old.

If there was no development on that property, then there was no reason to put a road up there. In fact, the owners of the property might have fought it—particularly if they used the undeveloped land for hunting or other outdoor activities.

He grabbed the surveillance photographs, thumbing through them, looking at the marks Hensen or someone had made that showed where this was located on the grid.

The satellite photographs showed a heavily wooded area, filled in with young trees. The county road ran along the bottom of the photograph. That road was so badly maintained that potholes were visible.

Several fire lanes and driveways opened onto the county road. Through the trees, Lex could see the brown roofs of several buildings, all of them far enough from each other that they would seem isolated.

His mouth was dry, and the eggs Benedict churned in his stomach. He regretted them now. Or maybe it was the coffee that caused him to be unsettled.

Or maybe just the information itself.

He opened the top drawer of the desk, saw that it was empty except for a few pens, and cursed. Of course it was empty. This wasn't his desk from home. He punched the intercom, and said to Mrs. Anderson, "Get me a magnifying glass. Quickly."

She yessirred him, but he ignored it. He held all of the satellite photographs of that region up to the light, dismissing one after another, until he settled on the one whose place on the grid matched the map he'd found.

Something reflected morning light—something shiny and metal. A tin roof? They weren't uncommon in buildings finished during the thirties, forties and fifties, especially in rural locations. He squinted, saw overgrowth thick and so abundant that he could barely see past it.

He set the photograph on the blotter, got the photograph of an area adjacent to it, and slid it into place. There was a fire lane off the county road that might lead to the shiny thing, but he couldn't tell. The fire lane had been poorly maintained. Obviously, there hadn't been a lot of traffic on it—which made sense if the land was owned by J. B. Bynes.

Mrs. Anderson came into the office, clutching a magnifying glass. She set it on his desk and left without saying a word, something Lex appreciated.

He picked up the glass and ran it over the satellite photograph. The flash of light bounced off the roof of something smaller than a building. A truck, maybe, or a car.

Next to it was something he wouldn't have noticed without the magnifying glass. A moss-covered brown roof. Without the glass, it had looked like part of the woods.

"Found you, you son of a bitch," Lex said. "I finally found you."

CHAPTER SIXTEEN

The phone call came in two hours later.

Lex had spent the morning sending out people to gather more information. He told the FBI guys just enough to get them out of his way. And then he assembled his own security team.

He was going to get his father, and deal with J. B. Bynes his own way.

Mrs. Anderson intercommed him just before he went back to the Club Noir to meet with the guys—old friends all—who were going to go with him.

"Mr. Luthor," she said in a tone of voice he'd only heard people use with his father. "You have a call."

As she said that, the door to his office opened and Hensen stood there.

"We think it's him," Hensen said.

"Then you should have him," Lex said. "You can trace anything nowadays."

"Except cell phones. We're not getting a reading yet, which leads me to believe this is one, but we will. If nothing else, we'll triangulate the signal."

"I thought you have to be close to do that," Lex said.

"We will," Hensen said. "Once we pinpoint the tower he's using, we'll get someone there to triangulate."

Lex resisted the urge to roll his eyes. He was so glad he wasn't one of those people who listened to authority and trusted their every word. If he did, he knew his father would die at these kidnappers' hands.

No wonder Dewitt the Expert had such an abysmally poor

success rate. Attempting to triangulate a signal that could be coming from California for all they knew.

As if that would work.

"All right," Lex said. "You can leave now."

"I'm going to help you with the call," Hensen said.

"No, you're not." Lex put his hand on the receiver. "I'll risk letting him hang up before I talk in front of you."

Hensen's mouth thinned. In that moment, Lex realized that Hensen approved of him even less than Dewitt had. Hensen just hid it better.

But Hensen backed out of the door, and Lex picked up the receiver, punching the button for the line at the same time.

"Lex Luthor."

"Took you long enough." The voice was vaguely familiar, but Lex didn't know if that was because he expected it to be. He wondered what J. B. Bynes would do if Lex called him by name.

But Lex decided not to. He didn't want to scare the man off. "Do I know you?" Lex asked, his tone cold.

"Do you know me." The man laughed. "Good one. Nice try, Lex, old chum. You know exactly who I am, and you're toying with me, trying to keep me on the line so that your police buddies can trace this call. Tell them it's not worth their time. I'm not using a tower. I got one of them satellite phones—"

Something people often needed in wooded areas, because there weren't cell towers close enough, or the reception was too bad to use.

"—and they're not going to be able to track me down, ever."

"I see," Lex said, not surprised by this development. Bynes had shown amazing savvy thus far. That had surprised Lex, although it shouldn't have. Bynes had been a smart man. Lex still wondered if Bynes had planned this long before he even came to Smallville.

"You do, huh?" Bynes—or one of his henchmen—said.

"What I don't understand," Lex said, "is why you didn't e-mail me this time."

"Figured I only got one free pass at your friend's Internet café. Did I photograph real good? I tried to give you the best view of my nostril that I could."

So he had seen the small camera on top of the computer. But he hadn't known about the one behind the desk. Lex was going to keep it that way.

"Your pores need flushing," Lex said. "They're a bit enlarged."

"I'll do it when I got the money," Bynes said. "You are going to get me the money, aren't you?"

"You haven't told me when you want it." Lex picked up the satellite photograph. If Bynes was using a satellite phone, then he could be calling from this little spot in the woods right now.

"I figured you were smart enough to know I'd want it as soon as possible."

"You going to come here and get it?" Lex asked.

Bynes let out a bark of a laugh. "Nice try. I've got instructions for you. Ready to take them down?"

"No, actually." Lex leaned back in his chair, pretending to be relaxed, just like he would if he were talking to Bynes in person.

His words met with silence on the other end, and for a long moment, Lex thought Bynes had hung up. Then Bynes said, "No?"

"No."

"So it is true. You really do hate your father."

"How I feel about my father is between me and him," Lex

said. "What I am unwilling to do is pay you money if you've already murdered him."

Lex regretted that phrasing immediately. *If you've already murdered him* left the door open for Lex paying Bynes, and then Bynes killing his father. In fact, it almost put the idea into Bynes head.

"He's alive," Bynes said.

"I have no proof of that," Lex said. "All you sent me were some photos taken shortly after you kidnapped him and a video taken God knows when. I've had nothing today. For all I know, you're not even the guy who has him."

"I'm the guy." Bynes sounded offended.

"There's no way for me to know that," Lex said. "Your *modus operandi* is different."

"My what?"

Lex smiled. "Your way of doing things," he said, making his tone deliberately condescending.

"You and your father have a lot in common, you know that?"

"Of course we do," Lex said. "He raised me, after all."

Bynes made a noise that sounded suspiciously like a Bronx cheer. "You want the instructions or not?"

"You can give them to me," Lex said, "but I won't follow them until I have definitive proof that my father is alive right now, as we speak."

"And if I can't provide that?"

Lex's entire body turned cold. He gripped the phone so hard that he could feel the plastic give. "Then you don't get your money."

"And you don't get your father back," Bynes said.

Lex took a deep breath, doing his best to sound calm. "If you kill him, we both lose."

"Do we?" Bynes asked. "Seems to me you stand to inherit a lot. You could share, you know."

Lex slammed down the phone, hoping he made the right choice. His father always told him not to negotiate with terrorists, kidnappers, or any other criminal who crossed his path. *It's always the wrong decision, Lex. They'll keep coming back.*

Still, hearing his father's voice on this did not reassure him. It made him feel worse.

He was gambling with his father's life. He knew it, and now Bynes knew it, but probably didn't understand why. If his father was alive now, he might not be shortly.

Or Bynes might call Lex's bluff and send photographs, something to prove that his father was alive.

Lex hid his face in his hands. He wouldn't wait for another contact.

He had to move quickly. He had no other choice.

Clark was on his way to American history class when he glanced out the windows in the hallway and saw a blond head bob through the cars in the parking lot. Chloe. She wasn't going to wait for lunch.

He should have known. She was too obsessed by this. She wanted the story too much.

He wondered where she was going. He had told her that he knew how to find out who had been laid off.

But of course Chloe had her sources, too, and she was going to talk to all of them—without him. Then she would go and get into trouble, and he wouldn't be able to save her. Not without knowing where she was.

"What's going on?" Pete stopped right in front of Clark. Lana was just behind him.

"Chloe. I promised to help her with the story, and she's leaving now."

"Now?" Lana asked. "We've got most of the school day to finish."

Clark nodded. "Look, I'm going to see if I can stop her—"

"You won't be able to stop her," Pete said.

"Well, then, I'll tag along," Clark said. "Make some excuses for us, Lana. Say that I had to drive her home sick or something."

"Clark," Lana said. "You shouldn't—"

"Me, too," Pete said.

"If you're all going, I'm going," Lana said.

Clark felt his heart sink. He couldn't keep an eye on everyone. "Look, guys. I don't think there's any reason for this."

"We're all involved, Clark," Lana said.

Pete was already heading to the exit near the windows. "I'll stop Chloe."

Clark bit his tongue. It would have been more effective for him to do it, especially since she had such a head start, but now he wouldn't get the chance.

He had no choice but to trail after Pete. Lana followed.

"It would be better if you just made excuses for us," Clark said.

"Not for me," Lana said. "It's better to be doing something than sitting around learning about people who did something."

Clark shook his head, holding the door open for her as she stepped outside. "Somehow I'm thinking you meant for that to make sense."

"You know what I mean, Clark."

And he did, too. That was the tough part. He let the door close behind them.

The air had a bit of a chill to it today. The heat from the previous days was gone. Clark started across the sidewalk, heading for the parking lot, tempted to take large steps so that he left Lana behind.

But she managed to keep pace with him. She seemed as determined as Chloe did.

Pete was already halfway across the parking lot, running and waving his arms. Chloe had driven toward the entrance, but she stopped, apparently having seen Pete. She stopped there, rolling her window down.

Clark could hear her voice, even though he was still half a parking lot away.

"You're not going to change my mind. I've got a lead . . ."

And then her voice faded. She must have turned her head. Pete walked to the side of the car. He was responding to her, but Clark couldn't hear him.

Then Pete grabbed the car door and pulled it open. He stood there, not getting in, and looked for Clark.

"Come on," Lana said. She ran between a group of cars until she reached Chloe.

Clark followed, wishing that there was some other way to do this. He knew it would be better to wait, but no one else was going to.

And he had a bad feeling about the entire project.

When he reached the car, Lana and Pete were already in the backseat. He looked at the passenger seat, remembering how his knees banged against the dashboard on the last trip.

"Get in, Clark, before Principal Kwan comes out here and I get into even more trouble," Chloe said.

Clark climbed in. "I'm pretty sure you're going to be in trouble anyway."

"So," Chloe said, as she took her foot off the brake, "where're we going?"

Clark pulled the car door closed. "You looked like you knew."

"I was heading for the plant. I figured I could wheedle the

names out of someone. But you said you knew a person who could talk to us." Chloe looked at him. "You weren't just saying that to keep me in class, were you?"

He could have lied at that moment, although he wasn't sure it would have done any good. She was already out of class, already in her car, already determined. And she had a plan in case Clark didn't come through.

"His name is Bob Reasoner," Clark said. "He used to work at the feed and seed. Then he went to work for Luthor-Corp. Now he's working at the gas station downtown. I saw him the other day, and commented on his new job. He said he was one of the unlucky guys who got laid off."

Chloe gave Clark a brilliant smile. "I knew you'd come through for me."

"It might be for nothing," Clark said.

"If so, then we'll all be back in class in an hour or two," she said.

Clark doubted that they would be back at all today.

CHAPTER SEVENTEEN

Chloe drove down back streets to an apartment complex she hadn't even realized existed. She had never been in this part of Smallville. Nor, from their comments, had Pete and Lana.

Clark was being unusually quiet—even for him. He had gotten out of the car with her at the gas station so that they could talk to Bob Reasoner. Reasoner was a short, dumpy man with a perpetually bitter expression on his face, certainly not someone Chloe would have expected Clark to know.

Reasoner had also been rude when he found out why they were there.

"Look," he'd said. "I saw where talking about this got Jed Franklin. I'm not going to tell you nothing."

"You think Mr. Franklin killed his family because he was laid off?" Chloe asked.

Reasoner had given her a how-dumb-are-you look. "I think Franklin got mixed up with the wrong element, and when he tried to talk about it, things got worse."

"What do you mean?" Clark asked.

"I said, Clark, I ain't gonna talk about it, and I mean it."

Clark had given him that gruff apologetic look that Clark seemed to specialize in, then he'd walked back to the car. Chloe had stayed for an extra minute. Sometimes Clark's aw-shucks style was too soft for people like Reasoner.

"I'm going to find out what the problem is, Mr. Reasoner," Chloe said. "And when I do, I'm going to put your name in the *Torch* along with everyone else's. So you can talk to me now, or you can talk later, maybe to reporters from bigger papers, like the *Daily Planet*. It's up to you."

Reasoner's eyes narrowed when she had said that. "You ain't as nice as you look, are you, Missy?"

Chloe gave him a half smile. "Not even close."

He sighed. "I'll tell you one thing, then you'll leave me alone. You won't mention my name, not now, not never. Got that?"

"Depends on what you tell me, Mr. Reasoner."

He seemed to weigh that. Then he started talking. "The problem started when a guy by the name of J. B. Bynes signed on at the plant. Troublemaker from the start. He tried to unionize, but I never thought his heart was in it, you know? He spent too much time talking about how much money the Luthors was worth, and how we deserved a piece of it. I think word got to Daddy Luthor, and those of us who was listening to Bynes, we all got fired."

"I thought you were laid off," Chloe said.

"Laid off is fired with benefits. We was told if we went quiet, we'd get the benefits."

"Mr. Franklin wasn't quiet."

"Nope. I think if word of that got back to Old Man Luthor, there'd've been trouble. But now even Luthor's got trouble, don't he?"

Chloe frowned. "You think that's related?"

"I think I done said enough, Missy." Reasoner turned his back on her and walked away.

"Mr. Reasoner," Chloe said. "One more thing. Where can I find J. B. Bynes?"

Reasoner stopped, and looked around as if he wanted to make sure no one else heard her ask the question. Then he walked all the way back to her.

"He's got an apartment on Oak Circle in that complex they built about fifteen years ago. Ground floor, first building, first apartment. You can't miss it." Then Reasoner had leaned close to Chloe. "I never did see you. I don't know you, and if you tell anyone you heard this from me, I'm gonna say that you're lying. You got that?"

He had actually unnerved her, not because she was afraid he would hurt her, but because he seemed so very frightened.

"I got it," she had said, and hurried back to the car.

At that point, she had offered to drive the group back to school, but they wouldn't hear of it. They made her tell about her conversation with Reasoner, and only Clark thought it sounded really strange.

In fact, that was when he went all strong-and-silent type on her.

"What's with you, Clark?" she said, as they approached the apartment complex.

Clark shook his head.

"Clark," Lana said. "You're being mysterious."

Usually when Lana butted in, Chloe got a little annoyed. But she was grateful this time.

Clark turned toward Lana. "I don't mean to be."

"Then what's bugging you?" Pete asked.

Clark shrugged and looked out the passenger window again. Trees that were half the size of the ones near the Kent farm grew near the curb.

Chloe willed him to answer.

"If it's that Reasoner guy," Chloe said, "I think he was just being dramatic. Guys like that—"

"Guys like that are usually straight up and honest, Chloe." Clark sounded almost annoyed at her. "I've never seen him like that, and I've known him for years. He never says much, but when he does, you listen."

Chloe sighed. "I did listen, Clark. That's why we're here."

She turned into the apartment complex's parking lot. The complex was one of those two-story things, with the lower apartments jutting out. The second-floor apartments had balconies that overhung the entrances to the first floor.

When it had been built, it was probably the best complex in Smallville. Since then, it had become run-down. So, apparently, had the residents. The cars parked in the marked spaces were several years old, dented, and rust covered.

Chloe stopped in front of the first building, just like Reasoner had told her to. She was surprised to note that two-car garages were attached to the buildings.

"I'm going to do this," she said. "I think it'll freak this guy if all four of us go to the door."

"You're not going alone," Clark said.

Chloe glanced around at Lana and Pete, who were both nodding.

She had known he was going to say that. In fact, she was counting on it. Even though she didn't want to admit it to the group, Reasoner's comments had bothered her, too.

"All right," she said. "Just you, Clark."

She grabbed her tape recorder and stuck it in the pocket of her jeans. Then she picked up her camera. Clark was out of the car before she was.

He met her on the curb. Together they walked toward the first apartment, leaving Pete and Lana watching intently from the car.

Small, neglected shrubs lined the walkway. Tulips years past their first bloom shoved their spindly buds through the hard dirt. The steps leading up to the first apartment were cracked and filthy from the winter snows. Months' worth of advertising circulars had been kicked away from the door and left on the stoop to rot.

Clark went up first, peered at the name above the bell, and shrugged. "This is it."

Chloe took a deep breath. She shouldn't have been so

pleased that Clark was helping her. One day she would have to go to places like this alone.

But something about this apartment, its darkness and obvious neglect made her feel more uncomfortable than she had ever felt approaching an interview subject. She glanced at Clark, who raised his eyebrows at her, as if he were asking her if she wanted to go through with this.

In answer, she punched the bell.

An anemic wheeze echoed through the apartment. No other sound came from inside. Chloe punched the bell again.

Nothing.

"He's not there." A woman's voice came from above them. Chloe had to step back, off the stoop, to see who was talking to her.

A woman in her late twenties, wearing a bikini despite the afternoon chill, her face covered with sunscreen, leaned over the rail.

"Where is he?" Chloe asked.

"Looking for work, probably." The woman shrugged. "Said he had a line on some good money."

Clark, after staring vacantly at the door for a moment, stepped back so that he was standing beside Chloe.

The woman grinned. "Thought I saw someone else underneath this balcony. Who's your friend, sweetie?"

Chloe wanted to say that Clark was in high school and should be left alone, but she had a hunch she would never hear the end of it.

"What kind of money?" Chloe asked.

"I don't know. He's not the most chatty guy." The woman leaned even harder on the rail. It didn't look too stable. Chloe wouldn't have put that much weight on it.

"So do you know when he'll be back?" Clark asked.

"Probably not for a while. He left for Metropolis about a week back."

"That's where he had this job lined up?" Chloe asked.

"You know, sweetie, you act like it's my week to watch him. It's not."

Clark gave her the brightest smile Chloe had ever seen him use. "I'm sure, though, you overheard a few things."

He was actually flirting to get information. Chloe never thought Clark would do anything like that.

"Honey, if you come up here, I'll tell you a few things."

Clark's smile got wider. "You did, didn't you," he said. "What'd you hear?"

"I heard him fighting with one of his buddies. The guy was screaming awful things about his family and everything else."

"Jed Franklin," Chloe whispered.

Clark nodded.

"J. B. said everything'd be fine in a week or so. Then he come back here a day or two later, with another guy. They were laughing, and going on like they were having the best time. That's when I called down to J. B., and he said he had one job to finish, and after that, he was getting out of here."

Clark's smile faded. "He said that?"

"Sure did. Don't like that, honey?"

"Just doesn't sound like him," Clark said, pretending to know the man.

"Oh, it sounds exactly like him. Don't know him well, do you?" The woman leaned over farther. Chloe wondered if the bikini top would stay on. "Want to come on up here? I could show you a few things."

"I'll bet she could," Chloe said under her breath.

"I mean, a few things of J. B.'s." The woman said, glaring at Chloe. Apparently, she had heard Chloe's comment.

"No, thanks," Clark said. "I'll just leave him a note."

"Best put it on his truck," the woman said. "If he comes back for anything, he'll come back for that."

"Which one is it?" Chloe asked.

"The one in the attached garage. I'm subletting it. He owes me three months, too, so I'm hoping he gets back real soon now, or that truck is mine." The woman pulled away from the rail, as if talking about J. B. Bynes's truck soured her on the conversation.

Clark glanced at Chloe, who shrugged. She hadn't expected a dead end like this. For some reason, she thought she'd run into J. B. Bynes at his apartment.

Lana and Pete had gotten out of the car. They joined Chloe and Clark as they walked to the garage.

"What was that?" Pete asked.

"Someone with too much time on her hands," Chloe said.

They reached the garage. The garage door hadn't been painted in years, and a large chunk of wood had broken off the front, probably where someone ran into the door. The windows were soaped, and Chloe tried the regular door to the left.

It was locked.

"Now what do we do?" Lana asked.

"Guess we head back," Pete said. "It's another dead end."

Clark walked to the regular door. "Let me try. It might just be stuck."

Chloe hated it when he did that. He seemed to have a magic touch with doors, an ability to open them even when she was certain they were locked.

Sure enough, he leaned his body into the door, grabbed the knob, and the door opened as easily as if it hadn't even been closed tightly.

"Someday you'll have to show me how to do that," Chloe said as she walked past him into the darkened interior.

The garage smelled of old gasoline and mildew. There was another odor overlaying that, one that seemed both familiar and disquieting. Chloe took a deeper breath, but couldn't place it.

Clark came in behind her, followed by Lana and Pete. It took Chloe's eyes a minute to adjust to the dimness, but enough light filtered in from the soaped-up windows to allow her to see.

The truck certainly didn't look like something to come back for. It was old and dented, just like the ones outside. The difference was that this one had no rust on it, and looked like someone had tried to care for it.

"It smells like the marsh in here," Lana said.

"Thank heavens there aren't any mosquitoes," Pete said.

Chloe looked at Lana. That was the smell, exactly. The stagnant-water smell of the marsh.

"Chloe," Clark said quietly. "That's not J. B. Bynes's truck."

"How do you know, Clark?"

"Because," Clark said as he walked toward it, "that truck belongs to Jed Franklin."

Chloe took a good look at it. Clark was right; the truck was the one she'd seen in the police descriptions, down to the license plate.

The overhead light went on. Chloe turned slightly. Pete was still holding the switch, but he was looking at the floor.

Thick mud, still slightly damp, formed prints from two different kinds of boots. One set appeared from the driver's door of the Franklin truck; the other from the passenger side. They all went to the main door of the garage.

"Wow," Pete muttered.

"Wow is right." Chloe picked up her camera and took shot after shot, making sure she had enough light to get good pictures of the boot prints. "Don't anyone step on those."

"Two people," Clark said. "Two people came back from killing the Franklins."

"And they came here," Lana said. "That Bynes is involved, then."

"Maybe that plot thing my dad overheard wasn't so farfetched after all," Clark said.

Chloe worked her way toward the truck. She took pictures of it, too, the back, the sides, and the interior. Her flash illuminated papers strewn all over the seat.

"But we've hit that dead end," Lana said.

"I don't think so," Clark said. "The woman said Bynes thought he was coming into money. Maybe he's the one who kidnapped Mr. Luthor."

"And the Franklins found out about it?" Pete asked.

Chloe brought her camera down. The truck had a strong odor of mud and mildew and fertilizer. She fought the urge to sneeze.

"Found out about it, said they were going to report it, I don't know," Clark said. "Obviously, Mr. Franklin was involved."

"I didn't check the police reports this morning," Chloe said. "I don't know if they found his body."

"I'll bet they will if they haven't already," Pete said.

"All we have to do is let the police know that the truck is here," Clark said.

"Better make it anonymous this time," Lana said.

"I have a hunch if they find Bynes, they'll find Mr. Luthor," Pete said.

"Maybe I should let Lex know," Clark said.

Chloe was only half-listening. She reached through the open passenger window, and took a sheet of paper off the top.

It didn't look like a receipt for grain or gas. It looked like a scrap of writing paper, something someone would have in their kitchen for notes or scrap.

She held the edge of the paper between the nails of her thumb and forefinger.

"What's that?" Lana asked.

"I don't know," Chloe said. She carefully opened the crumpled sheet, and read:

Old County Rd. B about 10 miles to Fire Road 115423 (hard to see. Weeds). Turn right, follow 3 miles. Cabin on left.

"Directions," Clark said, looking over her shoulder.

"To somewhere obscure," Lana said.

Chloe nodded. "A cabin in the woods."

"The perfect place to hide something," Pete said.

Chloe shoved the paper in her pocket. "Or someone," she said.

CHAPTER EIGHTEEN

The country road was as filled with potholes as it had seemed from the satellite photographs.

Lex sat inside the cab of a flatbed truck—riding shotgun as it were—heading down the road at seventy miles an hour. The potholes felt like caverns at this pace.

On the back of the truck sat an elite unit of men, specially culled from various areas of LuthorCorp and from Lex's old friends. All of them were dressed like firefighters—the kind who took care of out of control brush fires. The flatbed truck, rented from a place just outside of Metropolis, looked like it belonged on these roads.

Now, if no one stopped them, the truck and its passengers would seem like men going about their daily routine. If they did get stopped, all hell would break loose.

The amount of firepower alone on the vehicle was enough to hold off most armies. Lex didn't have the clout his father had, so he wouldn't be able to make any police officer or redneck county sheriff look the other way.

And Lex didn't even want to think about the number of guys with shady pasts sitting behind him. These guys might just bolt if the police stopped the truck, and then where would they be?

Which was why Lex insisted on a strict seventy-mile-per-hour pace, which was fast for this road, but not completely out of line. Anyone seeing the truck pass would think they were on the way to supervise a spring burn or to put out something caused by the heat of the past few days.

If the passersby thought about the truck at all.

Lex was counting on that, not getting noticed. It was important to his plan.

His plan was simple. He'd go into the cabin with enough men and firepower, overwhelm his father's kidnappers, and get his father out of there.

Lex was not running this show, however. For that, he had a former Green Beret, who knew how to deal with situations like this. He had two sharpshooters, and several expert marksmen. If his luck held, the kidnappers would be dead before anyone even entered the cabin.

The truck bounced over several more potholes. There were no springs in the seat. Lex gripped his seat belt, glad he was inside instead of out. On the truck bed, the men were sitting on metal. They had no seat belts, and they probably got nearly bounced out of the bed each time the truck ran over something.

Lex was the odd man out on this trip. In fact, his men had suggested he stay back, that he might actually be in the way.

He would do the best he could to avoid being in the way.

But he had to be here. He had to see how this went. He was taking a gamble doing it this way, but gambling was the only way he knew to succeed.

Hensen had chewed him out after the phone call. Hensen had been listening on the other end. He was stunned that Lex hadn't taken the instructions, stunned that Lex had called the kidnapper's bluff.

But Lex hadn't told Hensen about this plan, and wasn't going to. When Lex left LuthorCorp's headquarters, he didn't tell Hensen where he was going. The FBI had been following Lex, and he would let them continue.

He headed back to the Club Noir, his cell phone on his hip like an Old West marshal's six-shooter. If the kidnappers called back, Mrs. Anderson had been instructed to put the call through to Lex, wherever he was.

So far, there had been no callback. That had him worried.

Hensen was checking Lex's e-mail, though, and perhaps the directions had come in that way. Or perhaps the kidnappers were having trouble finding a way to send more pictures and video without being caught.

The first time they had the element of surprise. This time, they knew people were looking for them. Going into an Internet café wouldn't be easy. Going home would be impossible, and setting up a line out here would be difficult.

Lex knew he had given them a hard task.

It also bought him time, and he'd been using that time as best he could. He'd sent one guy out here already to scope out the area. Lex wanted to make certain his hunch was correct before he committed men and resources to the rescue operation.

His guy had gone out as soon as Lex made the connection between J. B. Bynes's property and the satellite photograph. The man's instructions were simple: Make sure the cabin is occupied; see if he could see the occupants; and try to ascertain if Lionel Luthor was inside. The guy was not to attempt a rescue all by himself, and to pose as a hiker if he got caught by the kidnappers.

But the guy hadn't gotten caught. And he had found a bonus clue, one that guaranteed Lex was on the right track.

He had found the limo, hidden off the fire lane. The limo was parked in a ditch, covered with leaves and tree branches, and impossible to see from the road or the air. Lex's guy—whose real name Lex never knew—hadn't seen the limo either; he had literally stumbled into it.

He also took a few digital photographs of it, including the dirt-covered license plate. LUTHOR 1. That had convinced Lex to go in.

But he was being extra cautious.

He left an envelope with Mrs. Anderson with the instructions to give it to Hensen if she hadn't heard from Lex by four o'clock. Inside the envelope were the information and some of Lex's plans for the rescue attempt.

That way Hensen would know what was happening, that something had gone wrong, and would be able to send the real authorities in. They'd botch it up, of course, but if Lex had already screwed it up, the authorities' mess wouldn't matter at all.

The fire lane numbers were only a few digits off the lane he was looking for. Lex's stomach clenched.

"Remember," he said to the driver. "We block the lane about a half mile in, and then we go by foot."

"We don't know what the acoustics are up there," the driver said. "A half mile might be too close. They might hear us coming."

Lex had already thought of that. "Fine. They still have about two and a half miles to walk from the cabin to that part of the fire lane. If they decide to check us out, that's all the better for us. It'll mean fewer people guarding my father."

"I just hope they don't have this place booby-trapped," the driver said.

Lex felt himself go cold. He hadn't thought of that. "If they did, we wouldn't have been able to scout the place out."

The driver gave Lex a sideways look, but said nothing. Lex felt the contempt, but he ignored it. J. B. Bynes was a career criminal, not career military. He didn't do large-scale operations. Kidnapping Lionel Luthor was probably the most complex plan Bynes ever had in his life.

And, judging by Bynes's past, his henchmen weren't rocket scientists. They all probably assumed that the cabin was too secluded to find. They hadn't counted on all of Lex's contacts, and the information age's resources enabling him to find out so much so fast.

Lex put a hand on his cell phone. It still hadn't vibrated.

He hoped his bluff worked.

He hoped he hadn't made it too impossible for Bynes to collect the money. He had a hunch Bynes would be content just destroying LuthorCorp itself—which could happen without Lex's dad.

But those unknown henchmen. Lex knew they wouldn't be satisfied with some intellectual goal. They'd want cold hard cash. And if Bynes even mentioned that it wasn't possible, then the henchmen might turn against him.

Lex closed his eyes for a moment and leaned his head back. So many scenarios, and no way of knowing if any of them was right.

He was going with his gut, and he knew there was a good chance of his gut's being wrong.

Chloe had missed Old County Road B on her first pass. Only Pete's shout from the back seat had convinced her that something had gone wrong.

The road was no longer a major artery, and the sign was faded and pierced with birdshot. There was no official exit off the highway between Smallville and Metropolis, only an access road that led to a very active truck stop. Behind the truck stop was a road that ran perpendicular to the main highway. That road was Old County B.

Apparently B was one of those roads only the locals knew about. Potholes as big as craters made the road even more treacherous. A ditch ran along either side, so Chloe felt that if she swerved too much to avoid potholes, the car would topple over the edge.

"This is a great place to hide out," Lana said.

"Certainly is the end of nowhere," Pete said.

Chloe's hands stuck to the wheel. She was sweating, even though the windows were open and it was cool in the car.

Clark wasn't saying anything, having become the strong silent type again. Chloe had the odd feeling that he was planning something, but she wasn't sure what it was.

"Do we know what we're going to do when we see this Bynes guy?" Pete asked.

"We're going to ask him about Franklin," Chloe said.

"Chloe, how realistic is that?" Lana asked. "If he did kill the Franklin family, he's not going to tell us. And if he did, we could be in trouble just for mentioning it."

Chloe nodded. "We'll just play it by ear."

Clark shifted in his seat. His knees banged against the dash, but he didn't even wince.

"We're not far," Clark said. "The fire lane numbers are real close."

Chloe looked at him in surprise. She was beginning to get used to his silence.

Movement up ahead caught her eye. A truck was coming toward her, going very fast.

She hadn't seen any other car on this road. It made her nervous to see the truck.

"You don't think that could be them, do you?" Pete asked.

"Them?" Lana asked. "You mean Bynes?"

"Yes," Pete said.

"I don't know," Chloe said. "It's hard to tell."

The truck slowed, as if it were looking at lane markers, too. Then it almost stopped.

Clark glanced at it, frowned, and tilted his head. He looked surprised.

"What is it, Clark?" Chloe asked.

Clark shook his head slightly, and didn't say anything.

"Clark?"

The truck turned onto one of the fire lanes. As it turned,

Chloe noticed a lot of men in the truck's bed. Maybe six guys, maybe more. None of them looked friendly.

"What do you think that's about?" Lana asked.

"I don't know," Clark said, "but it can't be good."

"Why?" Pete said.

"Because," Clark said, "unless I miss my guess, that truck just turned up the road to Bynes's place."

CHAPTER NINETEEN

The fire lane was even more rutted than the road had been. Lex bounced along, feeling like his teeth would rattle out of his head. Dust rose alongside the truck. He was amazed the men in the back weren't coughing.

Lex turned his head so that he could see the odometer. He wanted to make certain the driver would stop at a half mile in. He didn't need to worry. It took almost no time to cover that half mile, and then the truck skidded to a stop.

The dust moved ahead of the truck in waves. Lex wondered if they could see the dust from the cabin, and if they could, what they made of it.

The muscles in the back of his neck ached from the strain. The inside of his right cheek hurt where he had bitten it without even realizing he had done so, and he was short of breath.

Behind him, he heard the scrape of metal against metal as half a dozen semiautomatics left the bed of the truck. Then the men jumped off.

Lex pushed the truck door open.

The men already had their heads covered, their faces painted so that they blended into the forest. They must have done that on the drive. He stuck out like a flashlight on a dark night. He could almost feel the sunlight reflecting off his very white, very bald head.

"My father comes out of this alive," Lex said. "You all understand that, right?"

They nodded.

He was just reminding them. He had already told them about the heavy penalties they would pay if any of them accidentally shot his father. If Lionel Luthor didn't survive this ordeal, it would be because he was already dead when the rescue team arrived.

Just like the directions said, the sign indicating Fire Road 115423 was hard to see. Mostly hidden by weeds, it looked like it hadn't been maintained for years.

"Stop here," Clark said.

Chloe stopped. Clark stared at the fire road. Dust still rose off it from the truck.

"We have to have a new plan," Clark said. "You guys are not going down there."

"You guys?" Pete said. "Since when are you different?"

Since always, Clark thought, but didn't say. He had slipped up and he knew it.

"Did you see what was on that truck?" he asked.

"Lots of guys," Chloe said.

"Dressed either like paramilitary people or firefighters," Clark said. "And they all had guns."

He wasn't going to tell the three others that using his X-ray vision, he also saw Lex Luthor in the front seat. Clark knew what was happening now. Lex had brought in a team to rescue his father—and a lot of people most likely were going to be killed.

But not if Clark could help it.

He got out of the car.

"If we can't go anywhere, what are you doing?" Chloe said.

"I'm just going to walk a little ways down the road, and see if I see anything."

"We're waiting five minutes," Chloe said. "You had better be back."

"Wait until I say it's safe," Clark said. Then he made himself smile at her. "Who knows? You just might have stumbled onto another story. Now stay here until I give the all clear."

She started to answer, but he didn't wait for it. He slammed the car door closed and headed off down the fire lane.

The road was overgrown with weeds and dirt. Most of the weeds had been knocked down recently, though, suggesting a lot of regular use.

Clark walked normally until he knew he was out of sight of the car. Then he used his superspeed to hurry down the lane, letting the world around him go into that superfocus that happened when he was moving fast.

He stopped behind a tree when he saw the truck. It was parked about a half a mile in. Eight men, most carrying semiautomatic rifles, stood near Lex. Lex looked nervous.

Clark understood how he felt. This was the choice Clark would have made if his father were in trouble. Not that he would have brought in men with guns, but he wouldn't have paid any ransom. He'd have tried to rescue his father himself.

Lex didn't have superpowers, so he didn't have the option of going it alone. He had to go in with help. Unfortunately, he had chosen help with so much firepower that someone would get killed—and probably not the kidnappers.

Chloe had been on the right track. J. B. Bynes had something to do with the Franklin family and with the kidnapping. More than likely the Franklins had died when they learned what the plot was.

Lex seemed to be giving last-minute instructions.

This would give Clark the opening he needed. Somewhere up this road were J. B. Bynes and Lionel Luthor. If Clark got there first, he might be able to prevent a lot of bloodshed.

He decided to speed past the truck parked across the road. The men would only see him as a blur. They would have no idea what he was. And it was better than tripping on things through the trees—and maybe forcing one of these nervous hunters to shoot, giving their position away.

He sped forward, hoping that this part of his plan would work.

Something blue and tall zoomed past Lex in a blur. A streak of light and color, zipping around him and the truck as if they weren't even there.

Lex wasn't sure he saw anything until the sound followed—the kind of hiss a car made when it carroomed past a person going more than two hundred miles per hour.

Whatever had gone around Lex had gone faster than that.

The team saw it too. They had their rifles aimed almost before Lex could turn around.

The rifles were aimed at him and his breath caught. Then he realized they were aiming the rifles around him, looking for the cause of the blur.

"Let's not get trigger-happy, gentlemen," he said in as calm a voice as he could.

"What the hell was that?" one of the men asked.

"Probably some kind of bird," Lex said. "There must be wildlife here. Let's not put a hundred rounds into a rabbit just because it startles us, all right?"

The men brought their rifles back into position.

They weren't as disciplined as he would have liked, as he even thought they were, but they were all he had. Now was the time to make the decision.

Did he let them go in, take that risk, and hope that they

did the job the way he'd planned it? Or did he abort and let the authorities take it?

Put that way, it wasn't even a choice.

"I don't want to hear any gunfire until we have Bynes in our sights, is that clear?" he said.

The men nodded.

Lex took a deep breath. Now or never.

He opted for now.

"All right then," he said. "Let's fan out."

CHAPTER TWENTY

Clark reached the cabin only seconds later. He stopped behind a parked truck, so new that its chrome still shone, except for the layers of dust on the mud flaps and wheel wells.

Two men stood on the porch. One of them was tall, with a beard, wearing a flannel shirt too hot for the weather and boots covered in marsh mud. The other . . .

The other was Jed Franklin.

Clark felt his stomach knot. Franklin was alive? He had killed his wife and children for this?

Clark couldn't believe it.

"What you're asking me to do," Franklin was saying, "is commit suicide. I'm not going to Metropolis. I don't know how to operate an e-mail, and I'm not going to ask someone for help, especially not when I have to add these pictures."

Clark turned his special vision onto the cabin itself. Two more people were inside. One was sitting down, head lolling to the side. That had to be Lionel Luthor.

"You don't go," the other man said, "and your family is dead."

A shiver of horror ran through Clark. Jed Franklin thought his family was still alive. He was cooperating with the kidnappers because he thought if he did, his family would live.

"What's the difference if I do this or don't?" Franklin said. "You already told me that if I get caught, my family will die. So you put me in an impossible position, J. B. If I don't do what you say, they'll die, and if I do what you say, I'll get caught, and they'll die."

J. B., so Chloe had that much right. J. B. Bynes was involved. No wonder Reasoner was afraid of him. Had Bynes threatened Reasoner's family, too?

Clark glanced over his shoulder. He didn't see or hear any of Lex's people, but that didn't mean they weren't on the way. He only had a few minutes to resolve this whole thing.

"Then you just gotta be smart enough not to get caught," J. B. Bynes was saying.

Clark scanned the entire cabin. There was a crawl space that went beneath the entire sublevel. That helped.

He needed priorities. The first thing he had to do was save Lex's dad. Then get Jed Franklin out of there. And maybe prevent the whole firefight.

He only hoped there'd be time.

"I don't like this," Chloe said, getting out of the car. "Clark has been gone forever."

"It's only been a few minutes, Chloe," Pete said. "It's going to take a while to go up that road. And you said you would wait five minutes, remember?"

"I hope he doesn't go too far," Lana said. "What if he gets seen?"

"We have no idea what he's walking into." Pete crawled out of the back of the car.

Chloe stared down the road. Nothing but wheel ruts, dirt, and broken weeds. No Clark, no truck, no mysterious J. B. Bynes.

"I'm going down there," she said.

"No, you're not," Pete said. "We're waiting for Clark, just like we promised."

Chloe sighed. Then she looked at her watch. "If he's not back in five more minutes, I'm heading down there, with or without you guys."

"If he's not back within five minutes," Lana said from the backseat, "we're all going down there."

So they were decided. And Chloe knew it was going to be the longest five minutes of her life.

Clark scanned the woods behind him, using his special vision. He could see seven people, heading toward him, guns in hand. They'd be here any minute now.

He ran using his super speed to the crawl space, and dug himself in under the house, then quickly turned around and pushed the dirt back so nothing would show. It smelled of mold and animals under there. He crawled over some mouse droppings. A spiderweb caught him in the face. He was in position, and it had only taken a few seconds.

"What was that?" Jed Franklin said.

"What?" Bynes said.

"I thought I saw something flash by."

There was a momentary silence, probably as Bynes looked, then the sound of boot heels on the wooden porch.

Clark held his breath and waited.

"I don't see anything," Bynes said.

Clark scooted into position under the floorboards. Using his X-ray vision, he could see the chair above him. The man in it wasn't moving.

"Look," Franklin said. "I'll do this last thing for you if you tell me where my family is."

"When you get back, I'll tell you," Bynes said.

Clark stuck his fingers in the cracks between the floorboards. Then he heard something that made him go cold.

The voice of Lex Luthor.

"Anyone in the cabin!" Lex's voice echoed over the valley. "You are surrounded. Come out with your hands in the air."

Clark scanned the area around the cabin with his special vision. Lex wasn't kidding. His men had gotten into position quickly and the cabin was surrounded.

The man inside the cabin scurried toward a window. Then, from the porch, came the sound of gunfire.

"What the heck was that?" Chloe asked.

"Gunshots, close by." Pete grabbed her head and forced her into the car. "Lie down. If we get hit by stray bullets, getting detention for skipping school is the last thing we've got to worry about."

More gunfire followed. Pete crawled in beside her, holding her down.

"You down, Lana?" he cried.

She didn't answer. Instead, Chloe heard the beep-beep-beep of buttons being pressed on a cell phone.

"Are you calling 911?" Chloe asked, thinking it was a bad idea.

"That seems to be my function these days," Lana said.

"They're going to find us here and—"

"Don't worry about it," Pete said. "I'm sure we're not the only ones calling."

"Besides," Lana said, "Clark's in there. I want help here if he gets hurt."

Hurt. Chloe hadn't even thought of him getting hurt. He seemed so solid, so indestructible somehow. But she knew it was a possibility. A very real one.

And all because she didn't have the patience to wait until the story came to her. She had to put herself in danger to get it.

Clark had said he admired that about her.

But the last thing Chloe wanted was for that admiration to kill him.

It sounded like World War III above Clark. Gunshots, over and over again, ricocheting everywhere, more bullets flying than he had ever heard in his life.

Above it all, Lex's voice, futilely shouting, "Stop! Stop! My father might be in there."

His father was in there, and he was in danger.

Clark, using his super strength, plunged his hands through the wood floor of the cabin above him, grabbed the legs of the chair, and pulled it into the crawlspace.

The chair fell on him in a shower of dust and debris.

Using his own body as a shield against any stray shots, he checked Lionel Luthor's pulse. It was strong, but the man was a mess. He'd been beaten and he was unconscious.

Above them, Lex continued shouting. Someone screamed, and Clark heard a thud. Then there was another thud, and the shooting stopped.

"You stupid bastards." Lex sounded more panicked than Clark had ever heard him. "If my father's dead, you'll all pay for this."

Clark wrapped his arms around the chair and the man in it, then, digging his heels into the dirt, pushed himself backwards, opening the crawl space as he went. As he did, he used his X-ray vision to look through the floorboards.

One of the men was sprawled near the window, another on the porch. The third leaned against the porch door.

Clark wondered if they were all dead.

He wasn't sure which would be better for Jed Franklin. Death or life. And he wasn't sure he wanted to find out what Franklin's sentence would be.

CHAPTER TWENTY-ONE

J. B. Bynes was dead, sprawled on the porch like a broken doll. The other man—who looked vaguely familiar—was propped up near the door, alive, one hand covering a wound in his leg.

Lex was shaking with fury. The cabin was riddled with bullets. He didn't care how good a marksman each of these guys was, they had screwed up just as bad as he thought the authorities would.

No one inside the cabin could have survived the gun battle.

No one.

He walked down the hill. One of the men he'd hired tried to say something to him, but Lex shook him off. Lex felt like he'd been encased in a bubble. He could almost feel his father's disapproval surrounding him.

It's amazing to me, Lex, that a son of mine is so very inept.

Lex nodded, almost as if his father had spoken to him.

Lex mounted the porch, stepped over Bynes's body, and ignored the other man who was reaching out to him. Lex pushed the door open and stared inside.

A single body sprawled beneath the window. It was too tall and broad to be his father's.

Lex started shaking. Had he been wrong? Had he led a firefight in this remote location for nothing?

It took him a moment to see the hole in the floor. He held his breath and walked over to it, peering down. Disturbed dust, fresh marks of something down there.

Had his father been kept underneath the cabin? That

wouldn't be the first time kidnappers had done something like that.

If so, his father might have survived.

If, of course, he was here in the first place.

Lex walked around the hole in the floor to the back of the cabin.

And there, on the weed-covered lawn, sat Clark Kent, untying Lex's father from a chair. His father was unconscious. Clark was holding him up with one hand as he untied ropes with the other.

Lex flung open the back door. "I'm imagining you, right?" he said, and he half believed it. How did Clark manage to show up every time Lex was in trouble?

Clark shook his head. "I'm real."

Lex walked down the back steps onto the lawn. Weeds grazed his jeans. In the distance, he heard sirens.

"Your dad's pretty beat-up, but he's alive."

Lex knelt in front of his father. He'd never seen the old man like this—hair filthy and tangled, blood on his face, his lips blue, eyes closed.

He didn't look as powerful as he should have.

"What're you doing here, Clark?" Lex asked.

"Actually, Chloe was tracking a story. She's just down the road, and I saw this truck come up here, so I was going to check it out, and—"

"Managed to rescue my father all by yourself?" Lex kept his tone light, but his face averted. He didn't want Clark to see how shook-up he was over his father's condition.

"No," Clark said. "He was tied up out here. I just knocked him over when the shooting started."

That, of course, didn't explain the dirt stains on Clark's back or the cobwebs in Lex's dad's hair. But Lex was going to overlook that for the moment.

The sirens were even closer now.

"You could have died," Lex said.

"If I'd known that," Clark said, "I wouldn't have volunteered to check this place out."

Lex smoothed the hair away from his father's face. It felt strange to touch the man. He so rarely did.

Clark stood. "I'll go see how Chloe and the group are."

Lex nodded, but didn't stand. He was reluctant to leave his father's side. Lex noted, with strange detachment, how unusual that feeling was for him.

Clark started to walk away.

"Clark," Lex said, turning slightly. Clark stopped. "I guess I owe you my thanks. Again."

Clark shrugged. "You know me, Lex. Wrong place at the right time."

And then he disappeared down the road.

CHAPTER TWENTY-TWO

Chloe put the finishing touches on the last of the news stories she had to write. She leaned away from the computer and stretched her arms. Her hands were tired. She'd worked through another night.

Clark had already brought her the morning coffee and a cinnamon roll. She could get used to this kind of treatment, although she didn't tell him that.

He was sitting in one of the chairs near the Wall of Weird, reading everything she had written. Lana was beside him, reading the pages as he finished with them and passing them to Pete, who sat cross-legged on a desk.

"I can't believe this," Lana said. "Danny Franklin is dead because this Bynes guy wanted the big score."

"That's what Mr. Franklin told the police, and everything Clark said he overheard at the cabin confirmed it." Chloe leaned forward, saved the story in rich text format, and then opened her e-mail program. This would be her first statewide byline. Not only was the story going in the *Torch*, but it would be in the *Daily Planet*, too.

That was the only way the *Planet* would get the whole scoop. She wasn't going to let them interview her. She had a hunch from the way the editor reacted, she'd be rewritten and her stuff would probably be turned into quotes after all, but she didn't care. She had her first shot at the big time.

"The poor man," Lana said. "Losing his whole family that way."

"He got in with the wrong people," Pete said, giving Clark a meaningful look. "Stuff like that happens when you think the wrong people are your friends."

Clark kept his gaze on the papers. Chloe wondered how he could ignore that look from Pete. "At least Lex's dad'll be all right," Clark said.

"As all right as he can ever be," Pete said.

"Pete, stop," Lana said. "The man's been through an ordeal."

"He puts the people around him through ordeals all the time." But Pete picked up another piece of paper and started to read, showing that this part of the conversation was done.

"So Bynes and this friend of his, Rowen, they kill the entire Franklin family, and tell Jed Franklin they'd been kidnapped just to get his cooperation?" Lana said. "It seems like a lot of work."

"I think they might have planned to kidnap them first," Chloe said. "I think the first death—probably Danny's—was an accident. The coroner said he fought his attacker."

"It also explains the two killer theory that we had," Clark said. "There were two victims each, and they took care of things fast so that when Franklin got home, he would think his family had been kidnapped."

"Why'd they need him?" Pete asked. "He didn't have any special skills. Clark said he didn't know anything about high tech."

"They needed someone they could blame when it was all over," Chloe said. "And he heard about the plot. Remember he was making a lot of noise about it around town. He became their victim."

"They had a lot of victims," Lana said. "Too many."

She bowed her head.

"We're all going to miss him, Lana," Clark said softly.

"I know," Lana said. "And it's funny. I feel a little better about it now that I know his father was trying to save his life, not take it."

"Me too," Pete said.

Chloe nodded. "Small consolation for Mr. Franklin, though."

"I doubt there's going to be any consolation for him," Clark said.

◆◆◆

School let out early so that those who wanted to could attend the Franklin funerals. Clark went, then decided to walk home.

As he came up the drive, he looked at the farm. He'd spent his entire life in the white house, spent most of the last five years looking at the stars from the loft, and spent the better part of a decade learning how to work beside his father.

It could all have been lost in an instant.

The family truck pulled up beside him. His parents were wearing their best clothes. They had just come from the funeral, too, although they had stopped at a neighbor's for the small post-funeral meal. Clark hadn't been able to face it.

"Want a lift the rest of the way, son?" his dad asked.

Clark shook his head. "Dad," he said, asking the question that had been on his mind the entire walk home, "if that had been us instead of them—"

"It wouldn't have been us, Clark," his dad said.

"Why not?" Clark asked. "Because of my strength?"

His dad sighed, then looked at Clark's mom. "You want to drive the rest of the way? I'll walk with Clark for a moment."

She nodded.

His dad got out of the truck, and his mom slid into the driver's seat, pulling away slowly so that she didn't spray them with gravel.

"Clark," his dad said, "Jed Franklin made one mistake."

"Going to work for LuthorCorp?"

"Forgetting he had friends and a community. If he had gone to the authorities the moment he heard about this plot, none of this would have happened."

"But he was afraid," Clark said.

His dad nodded. "But that's not an excuse, Clark."

"I guess not," Clark said. "But you heard him talk about this. You said it was crazy talk."

"He was drunk at the time. Doesn't help credibility, and neither did his bitterness toward the Luthors. He seemed to think they were going to get what they deserved."

Clark took a deep breath. He didn't like to challenge his father, but he couldn't let this one pass. "You've said that about the Luthors more than once."

His dad looked surprised. "Guess I have. And you know what? I'm beginning to think I was wrong. No one deserves what happened this past week. Not the Franklins, and not the Luthors either."

Clark looked at his father.

"You know," his dad said. "Times like these, a man needs comfort food. We never did finish those root beer floats your mom made the other night. Maybe we should see if we can get her to make some again."

Clark smiled at the twinkle in his dad's eye. "Sounds perfect."

DEAN WESLEY SMITH is the author of over seventy novels and hundreds of short stories, as well as a number of comic books and movie scripts. He wrote two original *Men in Black* novels, as well as the movie novelization for *Final Fantasy*. With his wife, Kristine Kathryn Rusch, he has written, among other books, twenty *Star Trek* novels. He has been nominated for every major award in the science fiction and fantasy field, and has even won a few of them, including the World Fantasy Award. He lives in a very Smallville-like town on the Oregon Coast.